P9-CFD-618

"I enjoyed your company."

Tony hadn't expected to say that when he'd opened his mouth. This was much too personal and revealing.

"So did I."

Whatever else Sasha might have said was interrupted by the insistent buzz emitted by his pager.

"You thought right, Henderson. Now call for backup." Tony closed his phone. His expression was sober. "They found another body."

She stared at him, her eyes widening in horror. "I'm coming with you."

"This isn't exactly according to the rules," Tony said.

"Neither is death," she answered softly.

She had him there, Tony thought. As he glanced at her direction, he wondered why he was really letting the doctor talk her way into coming along.

This Valentine's Day, add a little thrill to
your life with four new romances from

Silhouette Romantic Suspense!

This is our first month of new covers to go with
our new name—but we still deliver adrenaline-packed
love stories from your favorite authors.

This month's highlights:

- A doctor and a detective clash when *USA TODAY*
  bestselling author Marie Ferrarella kicks off
  her new series, THE DOCTORS PULASKI, with
  Her Lawman on Call (#1451).

- Meet two captivating characters with a shared past
  in *Dark Reunion* (#1452), the latest in Justine Davis's
  popular REDSTONE, INCORPORATED miniseries.

- Veteran storyteller Marilyn Pappano brings you a
  bad-boy hero to die for in *More Than a Hero* (#1453).

- Voodoo, ghosts and pirates? You'll find them
  all in *The Forbidden Enchantment* (#1454),
  the long-awaited sequel to Nina Bruhns's
  Ghost of a Chance.

Silhouette Romantic Suspense
(formerly known as Silhouette Intimate Moments)
features the best in breathtaking romantic suspense
with four new novels each and every month.

Don't miss a single one!

MARIE FERRARELLA

Her Lawman on Call

Silhouette®
Romantic
SUSPENSE

If you purchased this book without a cover you should be aware that this book is stolen property. It was reported as "unsold and destroyed" to the publisher, and neither the author nor the publisher has received any payment for this "stripped book."

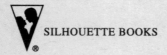 SILHOUETTE BOOKS

ISBN-13: 978-0-373-27521-2
ISBN-10:   0-373-27521-8

HER LAWMAN ON CALL

Copyright © 2007 by Marie Rydzynski-Ferrarella

All rights reserved. Except for use in any review, the reproduction or utilization of this work in whole or in part in any form by any electronic, mechanical or other means, now known or hereafter invented, including xerography, photocopying and recording, or in any information storage or retrieval system, is forbidden without the written permission of the editorial office, Silhouette Books, 233 Broadway, New York, NY 10279 U.S.A.

All characters in this book have no existence outside the imagination of the author and have no relation whatsoever to anyone bearing the same name or names. They are not even distantly inspired by any individual known or unknown to the author, and all incidents are pure invention.

This edition published by arrangement with Harlequin Books S.A.

® and TM are trademarks of Harlequin Books S.A., used under license. Trademarks indicated with ® are registered in the United States Patent and Trademark Office, the Canadian Trade Marks Office and in other countries.

Visit Silhouette Books at www.eHarlequin.com

Printed in U.S.A.

MARIE FERRARELLA

This *USA TODAY* bestselling and RITA® Award-winning author has written over 175 books for Silhouette Books, some under the name Marie Nicole. Her romances are beloved by fans worldwide. Check out her Web site at www.marieferrarella.com.

To Dr. Tonia Marralle, who delivered my children and gave me an idea to work with.

Chapter 1

There was something about a parking structure that always made her feel vulnerable. In broad daylight, she found them somewhat confusing. Most of the time she had too many things on her mind. Squeezing in that extra piece of information which identified where she had left her vehicle was usually one piece too many. Finding her car when that happened turned into an ordeal that lasted for what felt like an eternity.

At night, when there were fewer vehicles housed within this particular parking structure, she felt exposed, helpless.

And déjà vu haunted her.

It was a completely irrational reaction, she was the first to acknowledge it as such. But it changed nothing.

She wanted to run, but chose to move slowly, retracing steps she'd taken thirteen hours ago, when her day at Patience Memorial Hospital had begun. The lighting down on this level was poor. One of the bulbs was out, leaving the resulting shadows to threaten one another.

The air felt heavy and clammy, much like the day had been. Typical New York City autumn, Sasha thought. She picked up her pace, making her way toward where she thought she remembered leaving her car, a small vintage Toyota that had seen more than a handful of design changes come and go.

Dr. Sasha Pulaski stripped off her sweater and slung it over her arm, stifling a yawn. She felt exhausted. By rights, she should have left for the apartment she shared with her two younger sisters more than two hours ago. She'd actually been on her way to the elevator when Angela had called out to her. Angela Rico was a nurse on the floor, but more than that, she was a friend. Angela told her that the young woman who'd given birth less than two hours ago had suddenly started hemorrhaging. Sasha doubled back quickly. It had taken her less time to cauterize the tiny broken vein than it had to calm down her patient, who was convinced she was going to die.

But eventually, she'd managed to get the situation under control. By the time she left, her patient was doing much better and was arguing with her husband about the name they had chosen for the baby. A name, Sasha gathered, her patient no longer liked.

She eased out of the room before her patient or her husband could ask her to weigh in on the matter. As she passed the nurses' station, she saw that Angela had left for the night. Probably in a hurry to see her little girl before she fell asleep, Sasha mused.

Once upon a time, she'd thought that was going to be her life, too. Until the unspeakable had happened.

She forced herself to think of something else. Anything else before the loneliness took her prisoner.

God, but she felt drained. If she was lucky, she could be sound asleep in less than an hour. Never mind food, she thought. The urge for food had come and gone without being satisfied, fading away as if it had never existed. Now all she wanted was just to commune with her pillow and a flat surface—any flat surface—for about six hours.

Not too much to ask, she thought. Unless you were an intern. Those days, mercifully, were behind her. And still in front of her two youngest sisters. Five doctors and soon-to-be-doctors in one family. Not bad for the offspring of immigrants who had come into this country with nothing more than the clothes on their backs, Sasha thought. She knew that her parents were both proud enough to burst.

A strange popping noise sounded in the distance, breaking her train of thought. Instantly, Sasha stiffened, listening. Holding her breath. Memories suddenly began assaulting her.

One hand was clenched at her side, the other held tightly onto the purse strap slung over her shoulder.

She willed herself to relax. More than likely, it was just someone from the hospital getting their car and going home.

Or maybe it was one of the security guards, accidentally stepping on something on the ground.

Several people had been robbed in and around the structure in the last six months and the hospital had beefed up security. There was supposed to be at least one guard, if not two, making the rounds in the structure at all times.

That still didn't make her feel all that safe. The hairs at the back of her neck felt as if they were standing at attention.

As she rounded the corner, heading toward where she hoped she had left her vehicle, Sasha dug into her purse. Not for her keys, but for the comforting shape of the small can of Mace her father, Josef Pulaski, a retired NYPD police officer, insisted that she and her sisters carry with them at all times. Josef fiercely loved his adopted country, but he had no illusions about the safety of the streets, not where his girls were concerned.

Her fingers tightened around the small dispenser just as she saw a short, squat man up ahead. He had a mop of white hair, a kindly face and, even in his uniform, looked as if he could be a stand-in for a mall Santa Claus.

The security guard, she realized, her fingers growing lax. She'd seen him around and even exchanged a few words with him on occasion. He was retired, with no family. Being a guard gave him something to do, a reason to get up each day he had said.

The next moment, her relief began to slip away. The guard was looking down at something on the ground. There was a deep frown on his face and his body was rigid, as if frozen in place.

Sasha picked up her pace. "Mr. Stevens?" she called out. "Is something wrong?"

His head jerked in her direction. He looked startled to see her. Or was that horror on his face?

Before she could ask him any more questions, Sasha saw what had robbed him of his speech. The body of a woman lay beside a car. Blood was pooling beneath her head, straying toward her frayed tan trench coat. A look of surprise was forever frozen on her pretty bronze features.

Recognition was immediate. A scream, wide and thick, lodged itself in Sasha's throat as she struggled not to release it.

Angela.

Horror vibrated through Sasha's very being.

How?

Why?

She wasn't sure if she'd only thought the questions or if she'd actually said them out loud until Walter Stevens answered her.

"I don't know. I just found her like this. I think she's dead," he added hoarsely. Walter's watery eyes looked at her helplessly, as if he was waiting for her to do something about that.

Sasha dropped to her knees, pressing her fingertips against Angela's neck, frantically searching for a pulse.

There was none.

"Call the police!" she ordered the hapless guard.

Tossing her sweater and her purse aside, Sasha began a round of CPR that she already knew in her heart was useless. But she had to try because, despite everything she had been through, despite Adam's death, she still believed in miracles.

But there were no miracles for Angela Rico tonight.

By the time Sasha rocked back on her heels, finally giving up her efforts to bring the maternity-ward nurse around, more than a few of the people who worked at the hospital had gathered around her, drawn by the sounds of approaching sirens and the security guard's frantic call for help.

The murmur of voices went in and out of her head. Everyone was horrified. Angela had been one of their own. Everyone had always liked her.

In a daze, hating that it had already been too late to help Angela before she'd even got there, Sasha looked down at her hands. They were covered in blood.

Just as they had been once before.

With almost superhuman effort, Sasha fought hard to keep the dark shadows of the past from smothering her. Exhausted, she made no such effort to curtail the tears that came to her eyes.

Detective Anthony Santini was not very happy about getting the call that roused him from a sound sleep upon the sofa where'd he'd collapsed earlier. Today was supposed to be his day off.

On days off, a man could do what he wanted and what Tony had wanted to do was court oblivion. Especially today of all days.

Because today was his third anniversary.

Would have been his third anniversary, he corrected tersely in his head. If Annie were alive.

But she wasn't.

Annie hadn't been numbered among the living for the last ten months and nineteen days and the hole her death had created in his life just kept on getting deeper and deeper instead of closing up the way that know-nothing police shrink had told him it would when their paths had crossed. Involuntarily on his part. He placed no faith in shrinks. No faith in anything now that Annie was gone. All he had left was his work.

On days alone, he needed something to dull the pain and nothing seemed to work except a few hard drinks.

But tonight, his attempts to trample down his memories had been shattered by the phone.

Tony'd initially cursed at it, but it wouldn't stop ringing. Not until he'd finally answered it. Captain Holloway was on the other end, asking him to check out the homicide at Patience Memorial Hospital. The captain'd had the good grace to apologize, saying that everyone else was either busy tonight, or out sick.

Tony had felt like calling in sick himself, given the way his head was throbbing. But now that his sleep had been summarily disrupted, he knew that he wouldn't be able to get back to it. The best he could hope for was tossing and turning the remainder of the night away. So he might as well lose himself in his work. It didn't ease the pain that haunted him night and day, but it did give him a reason to go on.

Sometimes.

Pulling into the parking structure from the street entrance, he drove down the winding path until he saw the crowd of people clustering together and staring at something on the ground. Tony parked his car to one side and got out.

The crowd, judging by the uniforms and lab coats, were all from the hospital. He hoped that they knew better than to trample the crime scene. Holloway wasn't here, but he'd sent in several patrolmen as well as Bart Henderson, a tall, strapping man with fading red hair and a handlebar moustache straight out of another era. The man should have retired years ago.

There were times, like now, that Tony saw himself in the man's ruddy face. It didn't improve his mood.

Moving forward, Tony saw the body on the ground first. And the pale woman with blood on her clothing second.

Something about the woman brought to mind a line from an old fairy tale. For a second, it eluded him, and then he remembered. It was the description of Snow White. Skin pale as snow, hair black as night.

It went on, but he couldn't remember the rest of the description. However, from what he could remember, the woman who was standing beside the body could have posed for the fairy-tale princess.

Tony took out his badge and held it up as he approached. The crowd parted, letting him through, some asking him questions he didn't bother answering.

"Detective Anthony Santini," he told the pale woman. "You were with her when she was killed?"

His tone indicated that he made no final assumptions, waiting for her to answer one way or another. His dark gray eyes took precise measure of her, looking for some kind of sign, a "tell" as the poker players called it, to show him whether she was lying.

The woman's voice was low, soft, but strong as she replied, "No. She was already shot when I saw her. Mr. Stevens was standing over her—he was the one who found her." She took a breath, as if trying to put that between herself and the memory. "I tried to revive her. I'm a doctor," she added belatedly.

Tony nodded, keeping his eyes on her face. "Then she was still alive when you came?" It didn't seem likely, given that the victim was shot in the middle of her forehead, but he played along, waiting to see what the woman would say. "Did she try to say anything?"

Sasha moved her head from side to side, still trying to come to terms with what had happened.

"There was no pulse," she told him, her voice devoid of emotion, as numb as she felt.

"But you still tried to revive her."

She couldn't tell if he was being sarcastic, or just pressing her for information. "Sometimes, you can bring them back," she replied quietly.

The hurt was beginning to burrow its way into her. Death was a terrible, terrible thing. In her head, she could still hear Angela's voice.

I'll see you Friday, Angela had said.

Except now, she wouldn't, Sasha thought. Who was going to tell Angela's little girl her mother wasn't going to be coming home anymore?

"But this wasn't one of those times," she heard the detective saying.

Sasha looked at him sharply. But there was no humor, no sarcastic twist to his mouth. After a moment, she shook her head.

"No," she whispered more to herself than to the tall, dark-haired detective with the attitude, "this wasn't one of those times."

The woman looked, he thought, genuinely shaken up and he wondered why. Was she close to the victim? Did she know more than she was saying? Like the popular cult icon from a few years ago, Fox Mulder from *The X Files,* Tony's initial approach to a case was always the same: "Trust no one." Every word needed to be verified or supported before it became a viable piece of the puzzle.

Tony looked at the small, heavyset man in the

dark navy-blue uniform standing beside Dr. Snow White. A quick glance would have had someone labeling the older man a policeman. Only closer scrutiny would have taken note of the differences in uniforms. But there was one unsettling similarity.

"You have a gun," Tony observed.

One ham-like hand immediately covered the gun butt as if to acknowledge the weapon's existence.

"I've got a license," Stevens said quickly. "The agency pays more per hour for guards who have gun permits. And there've been muggings…" With a sigh that seemed to come from his very toes, Stevens's voice trailed off as he looked down again at the slain nurse.

Tony was aware that there'd been reports of people being accosted late at night in the hospital's parking facility.

"But none of them were fatal," he pointed out to the security guard.

"No. Not until now," Walter Stevens agreed heavily. Looking at the police detective, he blew out a shaky breath. "It's my fault."

Tony's eyes narrowed. Confessions didn't usually come this early in the game and in his experience, never without some sort of prodding and usually in trade for a lessening of the ultimate sentence. Taking that into account, he truly doubted that the guard was about to make life easy for him.

Drawing on his rather limited supply of patience, Tony asked, "How's that?"

Scrubbing a hand over his stubbled chin, Stevens rendered his confession. "I usually make my rounds earlier. If I'd been here five, ten minutes sooner, who knows? The nurse might still be alive." He looked down at the prone figure. "I might have been able to stop whoever did this."

Moved, Sasha placed her arm around the man's shoulders. At five-seven, she was approximately an inch taller than he was. "You don't know that," she said in a comforting tone. "Whoever it was might have shot you, too."

One of those, Tony thought, scrutinizing the woman again. A perpetual spreader of sunshine. Someone who felt called upon to lift burdens and cheer people up.

They had their place, he supposed, but preferably not in his investigations. Frowning, Tony focused on what was important.

"Why were you late in making your rounds?" The question was sharply asked, pinning the security guard to the proverbial wall.

If the attack had actually been planned, someone would have gone to a lot of trouble learning the guard's rounds and when he passed areas of the complex. For the nurse to have been slain when she was, it had to have been an unexpected attack, without any previous knowledge of the security guard's route. Maybe this was just a crime of opportunity and the young nurse had been in the wrong place at the wrong time. Or someone could have followed her without giving the guard any thought at all, which meant that he or she was unfamiliar with the hospital's policy.

There were a great many things to consider before they could feel that they were on the right path to solving the crime.

He looked at the guard expectantly.

"Something I ate," Stevens told him, pressing his wide hand to his less-than-flat midsection. "Been to the men's room three, four times so far tonight." He offered a sheepish smile. "Throws off my timing."

"I'll bet." Tony cut him off before the man could get more graphic. He glanced toward the doctor. "I didn't get your name, Doctor."

"Sasha Pulaski."

"Sasha," he repeated. "Is that Russian?"

"Polish," she corrected. "My parents are Polish."

He noticed, even though she still looked shaken, that there was a touch of pride in her voice. He wondered what that was like, to be proud of who you were, where you came from.

His eyes swept over the doctor and the guard. "I'd like to take you both down to the precinct for a formal statement."

Stevens looked a little uncertain about the turn of events. "If I go, there's no one down here to cover for me," he protested, concerned. "I'll lose my job and I can't afford to have that happen. I have bills—"

The guard sounded as if he was just getting

wound up. Tony put his hand up to stop the flow of words before they started.

"Henderson," he called over to his partner. The older man was consulting with one of the forensic investigators. "See if we can get one of the patrolmen to fill in for the security guard here until I get him back from the precinct."

"Why don't you just take a statement from Mr. Stevens right here for the time being? It might save you both a lot of time and effort," Sasha quietly suggested.

That caught him off guard. Tony thought about the solution she'd offered, or pretended to. He didn't like having anyone poke around in his investigation unless he asked them to, but the truth of it was, she was right. The patrolman could be put to better use canvassing the immediate area instead of taking the guard's place. And unless the guard had something significant to offer, such as having seen someone fleeing the scene just before the body was discovered, taking him down to the precinct would be a waste of time.

Mainly a waste of *his* time. In his experience, most security guards with night beats were not overly observant and spent most of their working hours just struggling to stay awake.

"Does that go for you, too, Doctor?" Tony asked, shifting his attention to her. "Do you want to just give your statement here and then go?"

There was something abrasive and off-putting

about the detective, Sasha thought. And he was doing it on purpose. Why? she wondered. Was he trying to create distance between himself and the people he considered suspects, or was he just trying to keep everyone at arms' length, in which case, again, why?

Had he seen too many dead bodies and had that hardened him, or had he started out that way?

She thought of her father. All the years that Josef Pulaski had been on the job, he never once allowed it to affect him, to influence him once he was home. She knew that her father had made a conscious decision to draw a line between what he did in order to put food on the table and the time he spent with the family he did it for. When he walked across that threshold and into their house, it was as if that other world where he spent so much time each day didn't even exist.

She supposed not all policemen could be like her father. And that, she knew, was a real pity because her father was a great cop and an even greater father, the kind who sacrificed his own comforts for his children.

"That's up to you," she told the detective, her eyes meeting his. She sensed that Detective Anthony Santini had no respect for the people he could successfully intimidate. "If you want to question me about what I saw just now, you'll find yourself on the receiving end of a very short interview because I didn't see anyone or anything—until I came up to Angela's car."

She'd set up an obvious question and he obliged

her by asking it. "And why did you come up to the victim's car?"

"Because mine is parked right over there." Sasha pointed toward the light-blue vintage Toyota.

He nodded. There was more and she'd left it unsaid. "And what would make for a longer interview?" he wanted to know.

"If you want to ask me what I know about Angela."

The way she said it, Tony thought, indicated that the doctor knew something. Whether or not that "something" was what had gotten the nurse killed had yet to be discerned. But then, that was his job, separating the fool's gold from the genuine article.

"All right." He looked at the security guard, making up his mind. "You can give me your statement here—for now," he qualified, then turned to look at the tall, willowy physician. "As for you, I think you had better come down to the precinct with me for that longer statement." The crime scene investigator stepped away, finally having gotten enough photographs of the dead woman. Tony immediately stepped forward. "But first I want to take a closer look at the body."

"Angela," Sasha told him. There was tension vibrating in her voice as he turned to her. "Her name is—was," she corrected herself, "Angela. Angela Rico."

Tony nodded, allowing the doctor her feelings even if he couldn't allow himself to have any of his own. Not that in his present state he even thought that he was capable of having any of his own. They'd all been burnt out of him the day he had to view what was left of Annie's mangled body.

"Angela," he repeated with a slight incline of his head.

Squatting down beside the inert body, careful not to disturb the pool of already drying blood, Tony noted that the young nurse's right hand was fisted. Had she been trying to punch her assailant when she'd been shot? It didn't seem very likely.

Tony narrowed his eyes, focusing. As he examined more closely, he saw that there was just the tiniest hint of some sort of piece of paper peeking out between the second and third knuckle of her hand.

"Peter," he beckoned to the investigator with the camera, "come here."

"Perry," the man corrected as he came forward.

Impatient, Tony ignored the correction. He tended not to remember names, only faces. "She's got something in her hand. Take a picture," he instructed.

The investigator aimed his camera. The shutter clicked twice.

Very carefully, using the tweezers he kept in his pocket, Tony extracted the paper from Angela's hand. When he unfolded it, he found four words printed on it: First Do No Harm.

Chapter 2

The frown on Tony's lips deepened. He turned his head slightly in Sasha's direction so that his voice would carry to her.

"I thought you said that she was a nurse."

"She was."

Was.

The single word vibrated in her brain. God, it felt so strange, using the past tense about a person who, only two hours ago, still had a future ahead of her. Angela had told her that she wanted to make something more of herself, to continue up the ladder, so that her daughter would be proud of her. Now, she wouldn't have the opportunity. And, at three, her daughter was too young even to have any decent memories of Angela. It just wasn't fair.

Tony continued looking at the note he held with his tweezers. Something didn't add up. "Then it looks as if our killer's confused. Correct me if I'm wrong, Doctor, but isn't this the first line of the Hippocratic Oath?"

Sasha looked over his shoulder at the paper the detective held up. Her knees bumped against his back, and something self-conscious shimmied through her. She took half a step back. "It is."

"Then why would the killer shove that into her hand?" Tony thought out loud.

"Maybe he didn't. Maybe it was something Angela shoved at the killer before he shot her." Sasha thought it over for a second. It made about as much sense as anything, she supposed. "Maybe that's why he killed her."

Tony rose slowly to his feet and turned around to look at the woman who'd been standing behind him with interest. "Do you know something, Doctor?"

She could almost *feel* his eyes penetrating her skin. As if he was expecting some sort of a confession.

She met his gaze head-on, refusing to give in to the urge to look away. "I know a lot of things. But nothing that'll do any good here." And that made her feel frustrated and helpless.

She had guts, he'd give her that. Most people looked away when he looked at them. "Maybe I should be the judge of that," he told her.

He glanced over to where the other detective was standing. The man had over twenty years on him, but the Captain had placed Henderson under him, a situation anyone else but Henderson would have been annoyed at. Not very much ever bothered Henderson. The older detective was talking to the hospital staff members who were clustered over to one side. Henderson didn't have much use for the crime scene investigators—said all the lab work got in the way of his gut instincts.

"You okay here, Henderson?" Tony asked.

Watery green eyes looked at him from beneath bushy eyebrows. "Haven't I always been?"

Sasha half turned her body so that the other detective couldn't see her lips. "He doesn't sound as if he likes you very much," she observed.

Turning the paper over to one of the forensic technicians for evaluation, Tony indicated to the doctor where his car was parked.

"Nobody does," he said as she fell into step beside him.

Sasha looked at the unsmiling detective, wondering if Santini was putting her on or if he was serious. His expression made her lean toward the latter, but she found it hard to believe that he would be so unaffected by what he'd just volunteered.

"Doesn't it bother you?" she asked, grateful to turn her attention to something other than Angela's body on the garage floor.

"No." Sparing her a glance, he raised one eyebrow in silent query. "Should it?"

On second thought, he didn't seem like the type to stay up nights losing sleep because he thought someone disliked him. "Most people like being liked," she pointed out.

"Most people *need* to be liked," he corrected. "It's an overt manifestation of insecurity."

"And you're not insecure." It wasn't really a question so much as an observation on her part. The man was the picture of confidence, and yet, there was no conceit evident. She would have said that was hard to pull off—until she'd met Santini.

"Nope." He opened the passenger-side door for her. "Watch your head," he instructed.

The words made her smile. It was something she knew that policemen said to the suspects they ushered into the back of their vehicles. Her father must have said the same phrase hundreds of times.

"Force of habit?" she asked.

He realized what she was referring to and shook his head. "Small car."

She was surprised that the department let him drive this little sports car. She waited for Santini to get in behind the wheel. "Regular car in the shop?" she guessed.

Starting the engine, Tony glanced at her waist, to see if she had buckled the seatbelt. Annie had never liked using it. Always said it wrinkled her clothes. In the end, it was her undoing. The first officer on the scene had told him if she'd used her seatbelt, there was a good chance she would have survived the crash.

God, but he wished he could see her just one more time, clothes wrinkled all to hell.

Tony banked down the ache and shoved it away into the darkness. He couldn't let himself think about Annie.

"This was my wife's car." She'd used his car that day, because hers was in the shop. He'd caught a ride to work from his partner. He should have insisted he needed the car and made her stay home.

Married. The man was married. Sasha tried to picture that and couldn't. Couldn't envision the man sharing himself with anyone. And, obviously, since he'd used the past tense, he was no longer doing it.

"Let me guess, you got this in the settlement." The moment the words were out, she regretted them.

A muscle twitched just above his jawline. "I got this at the funeral."

She'd never heard a tone so devoid of emotion. Or sound so incredibly empty. Beneath that emptiness, she had a feeling there was an endless abyss filled with pain. Guilt tightened her stomach.

"I'm sorry," she apologized. "I didn't mean to sound so flippant." Sasha spread her hands, feeling restless. "I do that when I get nervous."

She saw him slant a glance at her and it took everything she had not to shift in her seat. "Do I make you nervous?"

Sasha knew he was asking not as a man, but as a cop. She supposed he had to rule out everyone.

"No. But seeing Angela like that did. Does," she amended, since she was still fidgeting inwardly. "Everybody loved Angela."

"Obviously not everybody," he pointed out. "Someone killed her."

She couldn't bring herself to believe it was on purpose. Angela had never hurt anyone. But her purse was still beside her body, so robbery hadn't been a motive. If the killer *had* stolen Angela's purse, Sasha thought, he would have found very little in it. A single mother who doted on her daughter, Angela was always struggling to make ends meet. That was why she was hoping to become a nurse practitioner.

Sasha pressed her lips together as they emerged out of the structure. There was no moon out tonight, but the streetlights made up for it. "Maybe it was just an accident."

There was something in her voice that caught his attention. "You *do* know something, don't you?" He looked at her as he turned right at the end of the next block. "Was there an ex-boyfriend in the picture?"

"An ex-husband," Sasha corrected. Alex was his name. Angela didn't have time for a boyfriend. Her daughter and the hospital took up all her time. And then, because she knew the detective would find out, she added, "Angela had a restraining order against him."

"Why?" He fired the question at her before she was even finished.

Angela had confided in her and telling the detective felt as if she was breaking a trust. But death had changed the guidelines.

"Because he couldn't see his way clear to letting her leave him, even after the divorce papers went through. But he'd never hurt her," she added quickly. "Not like that." If you loved someone, you couldn't just put a bullet in the center of their forehead, she argued silently.

The light turned red. Tony looked at her, his voice steely. "What way would he hurt her?"

She remembered the black eye, the bruises that Angela had tried to pass off as clumsiness until she'd finally been convinced that she was setting a bad example for her daughter by remaining. "He hit her a couple of times. That's why she left him."

Tony nodded, doing a little math in his head. "Doesn't take much for abuse to escalate into something lethal."

Something in his voice sent a chill down her spine. "You speaking from experience?" she heard herself asking even though it was none of her business. She fully expected him to say as much.

He didn't.

"Yes." And then he looked at her as they came to another red light. "I'm supposed to be the one asking questions," he informed her mildly. "Not you."

She couldn't help herself. Ever since she'd been

a little girl, she had always pushed the envelope a little further than it was supposed to go, always wanted to know everything about everything. And to help if she could. It was in her nature. In her genes. Nothing had changed with age.

"Who did you abuse, Detective?"

"I didn't," he told her tersely.

And he never would. Not after growing up in a house where abuse was as regular as the seasons. Not after having his father beat his mother. He'd jumped to her defense, hitting his father over the head with a frying pan, then calling 911.

After his mother's death a few days later from the severity of the abuse, he and his brothers were propelled into the quagmire that was the state's foster-care system, moved around from house to house like unwanted pieces of furniture until his mother's Aunt Tess came forward to take them in.

"Your father—?" Sasha guessed, only to have him cut her off. More with his expression than with anything he actually said.

"I'm not one of your patients, Doc."

There was a warning note in his voice, a warning that told her if she continued to cross the line he'd drawn in the sand, there would be consequences to pay.

Instead of retreating, she flashed a smile. The first she'd felt capable of mustering since she'd seen Angela lying on the ground, dead. "You couldn't be. I'm an OB-GYN. You're the wrong gender."

"First time anyone's ever said that to me," he quipped.

Sasha glanced at Santini's rugged profile as he signaled for another turn. That, she thought, she could well believe.

Sasha sighed as she let herself into her small three-bedroom apartment. It was just a few minutes after one o'clock in the morning and she was beyond exhausted at this point. A second wind had come and gone and so had a third. At the moment, her energy was totally depleted, leaving her feeling barely human and incredibly sad.

The handsome detective with the permanent scowl on his face had wound up asking her more questions on their way down to the precinct than he actually did once he was at his desk and typing out her responses. In reality, there wasn't all that much more she could tell Santini beyond what she'd already said. What that amounted to was that as far as she knew, Angela Rico had no known enemies. Yet someone had deliberately killed her. Executed her, she thought, numbed by the thought.

Dutifully, she had given the detective the name and address of Angela's mother. Selena Cruz watched Rita, Angela's three-year-old, while Angela worked at the hospital. She assumed that Angela's mother might be able to give the detective information about Angela's ex, although she still didn't think Alex Rico could have killed his wife. If he had, he would have killed himself as well, because he maintained that he couldn't live without Angela.

Walking across the threshold, Sasha closed the door behind her. The single twenty-five-watt bulb they always left on for one another in the hallway cast dim pools of light on the floor beneath it. She yawned and sighed, debating just falling on her face on the sofa. Her bedroom seemed to be too far away.

A click vaguely registered in the back of her mind and suddenly, the apartment was flooded with light.

Sasha covered her eyes, blinking several times until she got them acclimated to the brightness. "You're blinding me," she accused whichever sister had turned the light on.

"My God, are you operating in the middle of the night now?" Natalya wanted to know.

Dropping her hand, Sasha saw Natalya coming into the living room, frowning at her. She and Natalya, eleven months her junior, shared high cheekbones and a passion for healing. Beyond that, they were as different as night and day. Natalya was shorter, with more curves and medium-brown hair that brushed against her shoulders. Her sister's eyes were brown, not blue, and right now, they were fixed on Sasha's clothing and filled with confusion and concern.

"Sasha, you're covered in blood," she cried. "What happened?"

She'd forgotten about that, Sasha thought. But before she could answer, another light went on, this time from the bedroom on the right. Leokadia, barefoot, her eyes half closed, stumbled into the room. The oversized T-shirt she had on indicated that of the three, she'd been the only one who had actually made it to bed tonight.

She didn't look any the more cheerful for it. "You two want to hold it down? Some of us are actually trying to get some sleep around here. You do remember sleep, don't you?" Kady looked accusingly at her sisters. "It's—oh my God, what happened?" Her mouth dropped open as she stared at her oldest sister. "Are you all right?" she cried, rushing toward Sasha. "Are you hurt? Whose blood is that? Sash, sit down," the petite blonde ordered, pointing to the sofa. "Can I get you something? Do you want—?"

In an effort to get her own word in edgewise, Natalya put her hand over her younger sister's mouth. She looked at Sasha, who everyone else had always regarded as the rock of the family. "Whose blood is that, Sasha?"

"Angela's. Angela Rico's."

Pressing her lips together, Sasha paused for a moment, struggling with her emotions as the reality of the situation finally sank in. The next moment, she offered her sisters a halfhearted smile of apology. At times it was hard to remember that although they all worked at the same hospital, Patience Memorial, or PM as everyone who worked there affectionately referred to it, they all had different areas of expertise. That meant that their spheres didn't always cross, which, in turn, meant that they didn't always know the same people.

She cleared her throat and tried again. "She was a nurse on the maternity ward."

Natalya nodded. "I've heard you mention her." Her voice was soft, gentle. It was unnerving for them to see Sasha like this. Except for when her fiancé had been mugged and fatally stabbed, it was generally believed that Sasha had nerves of steel.

Coming up on her other side, Kady placed her hand on Sasha's arm. "What happened to her, Sash?" she asked softly.

"Someone killed her in the parking structure."

Very slowly, her hand now on Sasha's wrist, Kady was drawing her over to the sofa. "Do the police have any idea who?"

Numbly, Sasha shook her head. Her legs seemed to give out from beneath her just as she came to the sofa. "I was just at the precinct."

"Precinct?" Natalya echoed. "You? Why?" she wanted to know. She was quick to become defensive and protective of her family.

"Because I found her," Sasha answered, her voice hardly above a whisper. The entire time she'd spent with the detective, she'd done her best to be clear-headed, sharp. But here, with her sisters, she let herself grieve. And it felt awful. "Actually, the guard did. Walter Stevens," she added. Neither of her two sisters probably knew who she was talking about.

She was the one who always stopped to talk to people. "But he looked so upset and confused…" Sasha slid her tongue along her lips, but they continued to feel like two pieces of dry sandpaper. Just like her insides felt. "I tried giving Angela CPR, but…"

Natalya took her hand. "You can't save everyone, Sash," she said compassionately. "Mama always says there's a time for everything, remember? A time to be born and a time to die."

A semismile curved her lips. "You start singing, 'Turn, Turn, Turn' and I'm leaving."

"I won't sing," Natalya promised. "Not tonight."

"You want me to draw you a hot bath?" Kady offered. When things got to her, she always sought refuge in a hot bath.

Not waiting for an answer, Kady was on her feet and halfway across the room, heading toward the bathroom before Sasha could open her mouth.

"Wait," Sasha cried. "Stop. Stop." Kady skidded to an impatient halt and turned around to look at her, waiting for further instructions. Sasha shook her head. "The way I feel right now, Kady, I'd probably drown in the tub. I'm too tired for a bath. I just want to get these clothes off and fall into bed."

"That can be arranged," Natalya said as she took her sister's hand and helped Sasha to her feet again.

Sasha felt a laugh bubbling up in her throat. It was a welcome sensation, even though there was such a thing as too much help.

"Thanks, but I can still undress myself, Nat. I'm not that out of it." She sighed. "It's just that…" Sasha's voice trailed off as her sisters looked at her, waiting, not wanting to interrupt. She dragged her hand through her hair, loosening pins. A few rained down on the light-gray rug. "God, what a waste."

Her sisters both nodded, even though neither one of them had actually known the dead woman. But each had already seen death, been touched by death's sharp talons, and knew instinctively what Sasha was going through right now.

Or thought they did, Sasha amended silently.

Right now she was just incredibly sad. And tomorrow, Sasha promised herself, or rather today, she amended, glancing at the digital clock on the coffee table, she was going to get up early and go to Angela's mother. She should have gone tonight, with that detective, but she couldn't face the woman with Angela's blood on her. But tomorrow, she was going to offer to do anything she could.

As if that could somehow help, she thought sadly. She felt powerless, and hated that feeling. Hated being imprisoned by it.

"If you need to talk, Sash," Natalya was saying as she began to leave the room, "you know where to find me."

"Me, too," Kady added.

They both meant it. They were both willing to give up their night to sit up with her, holding her hand both physically and emotionally, until she no longer needed comforting. Until the shock had passed and the pain was manageable.

Sasha could only think, not for the first time, how very grateful she was that she was not one of those poor souls who walked the earth alone. How grateful she was that she had her family to fall back on. Not just Nat and Kady, but Marja and Tatania as well.

And, of course, her parents.

Her wonderful, loving parents who always gave and never took. What would she have done if they hadn't been there for her when Adam had been slain eighteen months ago? She doubted very much if she would have been here today if not for them. They thought of her as the strong one, but they were her strength.

She looked from one sister to the other. "It's not that big an apartment. I'll find you."

Chapter 3

Tony leaned back in his chair. The frown on his lips deepened. Nothing. Granted, he'd expected as much, but he had still held out a smattering of hope.

The trouble these days was that anyone with half a brain now knew how to cover up their trail, thanks to all the different forensic programs on the airwaves. With everything but an intense, flash-of-anger crime of passion, perpetrators knew how to make reasonably sure that their prints didn't turn up on the things they'd handled while committing the crime.

And even with crimes of passion, if the suspect took a moment to think about his actions telltale prints would be wiped off.

Sighing, Tony stared at the crime lab report the tech had just delivered to him. The note extracted from Angela Rico's hand had only Angela's prints on it. To compound the disappointment, the note had come from a printer that had nothing remarkable about it to set it apart, no quirky imprint to separate it from the thousands of other printers he would find in the area if he were to look. The note had been produced by a standard color printer, not a laser, not the old dot matrix, which might have made things easier if the suspect had access to it.

And that was another thing, Tony thought, his annoyance growing. Their only viable suspect in Angela Rico's murder had an alibi. A substantiated alibi. At the time of his ex-wife's murder, Alex Rico was in Atlantic City, hoping he would have better luck at the blackjack tables than he had in love.

As it turned out, Angela's ex was a loser in both but no longer a murder suspect.

"Not unless he hired somebody to do it," Henderson volunteered wearily, ending a discussion that had been halfheartedly under way between the two of them.

They were the only ones in the immediate area. Everyone else, including Captain Holloway, had gone home for the night.

Tony glanced in his partner's direction. Together a little over two years, he and Henderson hadn't hit it off all that well. But then, to be fair, he hadn't hit it off with too many people. He preferred working alone.

Preferred everything alone, actually. Alone, there was no one else to disappoint you but you, he thought.

The notion brought a cynical half smile to his lips.

"If he hired somebody, what's the note about?" Tony asked.

The note bothered him. A lot. He felt as if it was pointing to something, but to what, he hadn't a clue.

Henderson shrugged his wide shoulders haplessly, the unironed shirt moving stiffly with the gesture. Without thinking, he scratched his neck.

"To throw us off?" he guessed.

Tony's half smile looked a bit sarcastic. "Alex Rico strike you as particularly clever?" Tony asked.

It was a rhetorical question. Still, Henderson considered it. "No, just grief-stricken. And mad. Very mad."

Tony thought of the victim's ex, and the rage that he'd viewed in the man's eyes, just behind the grief. "If Rico's innocent, we might have some trouble from him when we catch who did this."

"You meant *if*," Henderson pointed out.

"No, I mean *when*," Tony repeated.

Although he regarded the rest of his life with a jaded, negative eye, it never occurred to Tony that he wouldn't catch his quarry. Otherwise, there was no point in going through the motions. He'd taken the job, the badge, to make a difference. You didn't make a difference by not catching the bad guy.

Henderson nodded, backing away from a confrontation. "Cross that bridge when we come to it." With that, he switched off his computer and pushed his chair back. The legs scraped along the scarred vinyl floor that had long since needed replacing. The current budget couldn't handle it. "I'm calling it a night," he said needlessly. "Maybe something'll turn up fresh in the morning."

"Maybe," Tony murmured under his breath.

He scrubbed his hand over his face and tried to recenter his thinking. The pretty doctor had been right. Everyone had loved the victim. At least, everyone he and Henderson had talked to in the last week.

Pushing back his own chair, he began to rise when the phone on his desk rang.

"Looks like it might not be a night yet," he said to Henderson as he reached for the receiver.

Déjà vu.

It had never been one of Sasha's favorite words or sensations. As far as that went, it was way down on the list.

At the very least, it encompassed a teasing sensation that tormented her until she could finally recall what, where and when she'd done "this" before, whatever "this" might be. Most of the time, the answers to the questions that occurred to her never materialized as she struggled to recall an elusive memory that would put things in perspective for her.

This time, she didn't have to try to recall. The

memory that had sent the sensation rippling through her was still sickeningly fresh in her mind.

Angela, lying in a pool of her own blood on the concrete floor beside her car.

Since the discovery, Sasha hadn't stopped parking in the structure. It was either that or resort to taking a cab or some mode of public transportation. Although the city had probably the best public transportation system in the world, Sasha was possessed of an independent streak that fairly demanded she be in charge of deciding how she came and went. Subways and buses left you depending on others.

Besides, she loved that little ten-year-old Toyota. The vehicle had been her parents' gift to her when she'd graduated medical school. They could hardly afford to splurge the way they did, even though they'd bought it used. And, since they did buy it for her, not to use it would be tantamount to insulting them.

Entering the level where she'd parked this morning, Sasha realized she was holding her breath as she made her way down a deserted row.

She was too old to be afraid of the dark, she scolded herself.

It wasn't so much the dark that frightened her, actually, as it was who might be hiding in that dark.

Sasha glanced around to see if Walter Stevens was around somewhere. But if the security guard was on duty, he was making rounds on another level of the structure. There was no sound of anyone walking around here. No sound at all, really.

And then she heard it.

Every nerve ending in her body tightened as she listened.

A moan? A gasp? She couldn't make it out.

Sasha looked over her shoulder toward the elevator doors. For a second, she thought about running back. And then she became annoyed with herself. There were still cars here. Probably just someone going home for the night. Or coming on for the night shift.

"Hello? Is anyone there?" Sasha called. But even as she asked, she was hurrying over toward where she'd parked her car this morning before making her rounds.

There was a prickly sensation traveling along the back of her neck. It refused to go away, refused to be blocked.

And then she saw it.

Her breath caught in her throat, threatening to suffocate her. A scream escaped her, vibrating amid the trapped air. There was a figure on the ground, sprawled out like a mutilated doll. Like Angela, there was a pool of blood beneath her. Like Angela, there was a bullet hole in the center of her forehead. Her eyes were wide open, unseeing as they stared at the ceiling.

This couldn't be happening. Not twice. She was having some kind of hysterical hallucination, Sasha silently argued. Any second now, the figure would disappear.

But it didn't.

Legs no longer made of lead, Sasha broke into a run. But it was too late. The figure on the ground was not moving. The gray-haired woman had surrendered to death the moment the bullet had found her.

And then another sound came. The sound of screaming. Sasha did not immediately realize that it was coming from her.

She was never going to get warm again.

The iciness that surrounded her went clear down to her soul, despite the blanket that someone had draped over her shoulders.

Sasha was sitting in her car, on the driver's side, her feet planted outside the vehicle on the concrete floor as she faced the activity that was going on just a few feet away.

What were the odds? she wondered. What were the odds of this kind of thing happening twice? Two women, nurses, both shot execution style. And both times her car was parked close enough to the scene of the crime to be touched by the killer.

She shivered and took another long sip from the hot container of coffee the detective had shoved into her hands. It was half-consumed. Only belatedly did it register that he must have drunk out of it before he'd given it to her.

Whether it was meant to warm her hands or her insides, she didn't know. The no-frills coffee—black no sugar—failed to do either. But the jolt of super-strength caffeine did help her focus. Did help her hear his questions rather than just drift numbly away from the scene in a desperate act of self-preservation.

Her lashes felt moist. Was it the steam from the coffee, or was she crying? Sasha didn't know. She couldn't tell. Everything seemed so surreal.

"The hospital has signs up in the staff lounge advising women to go into the parking structure in pairs," she said hoarsely, more to the container in her hands than to the detective she knew was staring down at her.

"So why didn't you?" he asked her quietly.

The question surprised her. She had been referring to the dead woman, to the fact that if the grandmother of two had heeded the advice, maybe she would have escaped being the center of another homicide investigation.

Another homicide at PM.

It seemed absurd. They had above average success in keeping their patients from dying within their walls, whether they were brought here for surgery or because of some extensive illness.

But it's not the patients who are getting killed, it's the staff, a voice in her head whispered.

Why?

Sasha looked up blankly. The detective—Santini, wasn't it?—was looking down at her. There was a frown on his lips. It seemed like there was always a frown on his lips, she thought.

But then, murders were nothing to smile about.

"What?" she finally asked him.

"Why didn't you?" Tony repeated patiently, aware that she could be going into some kind of shock. "Why didn't you take someone with you? Why did you go into the parking structure alone?"

She shrugged. One side of the blanket slid down her shoulder. Tony moved it back into place, his fingers brushing against the side of her neck. They felt rough, as if he worked with his hands when he wasn't being a cop.

"It was late," Sasha replied.

"All the more reason," he pointed out. When he'd taken the call that brought him back to the location where he'd been just two weeks ago, canvassing the area, he hadn't expected to find the doctor at the center of the scene again.

The sensation that had shimmied through him was a surprise as well.

Sasha thought for a second. She supposed, to the detective, it must have appeared stupid. In hindsight, she had to agree. But she'd been going alone to the parking structure every night since they'd found Angela's body. Besides, she didn't think of herself in terms of mortality.

Sasha's hands tightened around the container. "No one else was leaving when I left and I don't like inconveniencing people."

His eyes met hers. "Murder is the ultimate inconvenience," he commented. Satisfied that the woman could understand him and process his questions now, he began by asking the obvious one. "Did you know the victim?"

Sasha bit back a sigh. She nodded. "Her name's

Rachel Wells. She's a nurse. And a grandmother."
Sasha suddenly realized where he was going with
this. "I didn't know her well. Just to nod to, that kind
of thing. She once showed me a photograph of her
grandchildren. It was a Christmas-card photo," she
added.

Santini gave no indication that he was pleased or
displeased with her answer. She didn't like faces she
couldn't read. Everything that any of her family felt
was right out there for everyone to see.

"Did the other victim know her?" he wanted to
know.

The feeling of helplessness swaddled her. She
hated being useless, but there wasn't anything useful
she could tell him.

"They were both nurses. I suppose they knew
each other, but I really couldn't say for sure." Did he
think there was a serial killer out there, focusing on
PM's nurses? She narrowed her eyes. "Why?"

"I don't know yet," he told her simply, even
though as a rule he didn't like having questions about
his methods being put to him. "I figure if we ask
enough questions, we might wind up finding an
answer that'll tell us something."

That made sense. Right now, it was difficult to
pull her thoughts together coherently. "Do you think
this is some kind of a serial killer, going around
murdering nurses for some twisted reason?"

He didn't answer at first. "What do you think?"

Sasha looked at the detective sharply, her mind

kicking in for the first time since she'd looked down to see her second victim in a little more than two weeks. Was he toying with her? Baiting her? She raised her chin slightly.

"I don't know what to think."

Tony inclined his head, as if in agreement. "Neither do I," he admitted mildly.

That was a crock. She didn't buy it for a minute. Detective Anthony Santini looked like the kind of man who knew *exactly* what he thought at all times. Moreover, he looked like a man who was on top of everything, be it situations or people, and he undoubtedly made it a point to remain that way.

And then she saw a spark enter his eyes. His interest seemed to sharpen, as if a new idea had just occurred to him. Sasha wasn't sure if she wanted to know what it was.

The next moment, she decided that she *had* to know what it was. If she didn't find out, she knew she would have no peace.

"What?"

Tony pointed out the obvious, straddling a fence, as if to see which side he was going to climb down on. "You found both bodies and both victims were holding the same note."

For the first time, she felt something other than grief for the victims and the family members who were left behind. Was he actually saying he suspected her of being the one who'd killed both women? How could he possibly even *think* something so stupid?

"The guard found Angela," she reminded him. "But technically, I guess you could say that, yes," she allowed. Her stomach felt as if it was on its way to meet her throat. Dear God, she hoped she wouldn't wind up doing something stupid, letting her nerves get the better of her. "Why?"

This doctor might or might not be the common thread here, he thought, since they had no other viable lead. It seemed an incredible coincidence that she was in the same vicinity as both of the victims.

"Do you know anyone who might be doing this to get your attention?"

It took her a second to absorb the question.

"My attention?" she repeated incredulously.

"You know, like a cat coming into the house and laying whatever they've killed down by your feet." He saw the revulsion enter her eyes. He'd thought doctors didn't become grossed out. "To them, it's a flattering gesture, not a sickening one."

Sasha pressed her lips together. Someone was killing their nurses and this man was talking nonsense. "No, I don't know anyone who would bring me dead bodies as a gift."

The ghostly pallor was receding from her cheeks, he noted. He was getting her angry. Righteously, or was that bravado? "You said you were a female doctor?"

How archaic did that sound? "I'm an OB-GYN," she corrected.

His eyes never left her face. "Lose any mothers or babies lately?"

Did he think some deranged husband or parent was killing innocent people because they were trying to get back at her?

"You *are* crazy," she told him, taking umbrage for her patients and their families.

He never batted an eye. "Part of the job, ma'am."

Tony glanced over toward the yellow taped-off area. As he'd instructed at the first homicide, one of the crime scene investigators was scanning the area with a video camera. He wanted to compare tapes, see if anyone who had come to the first homicide turned up at the second. Besides the good doctor here.

He turned his attention back to her. "I'm afraid I'm going to need you to give me a statement again."

She'd expected as much when she'd placed the 911 call to report the murder.

And then something suddenly dawned on her. "Do you think I did it?"

"I think everyone did it," he answered. "Until I can weed the non-suspects out, one at a time."

This seemed just too fantastic for her to absorb. That someone would think she was a murderer boggled her mind.

"Why would I kill Angela and Rachel?"

His eyes met hers. She'd never seen such serious eyes in her life. "If I had the answer to that, this would be easy."

"Then I'll give you an answer," she told him heatedly. He was wasting his time with this line of thinking and the sooner he moved on, the closer he would get to catching Angela and Rachel's killer. And maybe preventing another murder as well. "I didn't kill them. I didn't kill anyone. I don't even step on bugs."

There was just the barest hint of amusement evident. "Maybe you should. Their population is really exploding these days. Had to move out of my last apartment because the roaches reclaimed the building."

Sasha shook her head. "You're insane."

"So you already pointed out," he told her, unruffled. He took the empty cup from her and saw her stiffen indignantly.

"If you want my prints," she told him tersely, "you just have to ask. My DNA, too."

He laughed softly, humorlessly. "Everybody's a CSI wannabe." Glancing around, he beckoned over a policeman. "Sergeant, take the doctor down to the precinct. We need to get her statement."

"I can do it," Henderson volunteered, pocketing the small notebook he always used to take down information that came his way.

"I need you here," Tony told him. "I'll have a patrolman drive her in." He spared a glance at Sasha. "I'll see you at the station."

"Doesn't matter where you'll see me," she informed him, "the answers will still be the same."

He merely nodded, walking away to speak to one of the patrolman. "Good, means you're not lying."

Sasha felt a flash of temper. She opened her mouth and then closed it again, feeling it more prudent not to say anything until she had more control over what could come out. All she knew right now was that the detective was getting under her skin at an amazing speed and rubbing her completely the wrong way.

Chapter 4

"Can I get you anything?"

The voice came from behind her. Sasha twisted around in the hardback chair to see Tony approaching her in the squad room. She'd been sitting beside his desk for the last fifteen minutes, waiting for him to make an appearance. She couldn't help wondering if he was making her wait on purpose.

"A time machine," she quipped, turning back around to face him as he moved his chair out.

Tony sat down and turned on his computer. A low grinding noise began to hum through the office as it went through its paces.

"Why?" he asked. "How far back would you go?"

"Two weeks."

He looked at her. Two weeks was the amount of time separating the two murders. Was she making a backhanded confession?

"And maybe I'd start taking the bus to work," Sasha added, thinking out loud. "Coming across one victim was bad enough. Two…" Her voice trailed off as she shook her head.

Then she raised her eyes to his and Tony found himself thinking that he'd never seen eyes quite that shade of blue before. Intense. Beautiful. And pretty damn hypnotic if he allowed them to be. Mentally, he pulled himself back.

"I know you're overworked here and under-staffed," she said, edging closer on her chair, "but you must have some kind of a lead, a clue, a hunch—"

Tony regarded her with mild interest. People didn't usually attribute human frailties to the police department. They expected tireless, around-the-clock vigilance. And crimes to be solved in a timely fashion—as in yesterday. All the best crime dramas on television made it seem easy.

If only.

"How do you know we're overworked and under-staffed?" he wanted to know.

Was the man born antagonistic, or had he just acquired the habit along the way? She was trying to be nice here.

"Well, aren't you? Why should you be any differ-ent from the rest of the world? Besides," she sighed, sitting back again, "that's the way it always was when my father was with the two-six in Queens."

She'd succeeded in getting his attention, Sasha thought. The look in his eyes changed. "Your father was on the job?"

Tony noted the way she smiled before she answered. Pride mingled with memories. A family girl, he thought. He should have realized that. Because of his own situation, he had a tendency to think of people simply as detached individuals. He wasn't close to either one of his brothers, even though they both lived in the city and worked for it, Joe as a detective in Brooklyn and Tim as a firefighter in Staten Island. But for all the contact they'd had in the last five years, they could have just as well have been spread out all over the country.

"Twenty-six years," she told him. Definitely pride there, he thought. It was audible in her voice. "Josef Pulaski. He made detective before he retired."

Just like his father had been, he thought. Except that he was willing to bet that was where the similarity ended. If he'd ever been proud of his father, that had changed a long time ago—by the time he could understand what was going on behind his parents' closed door.

He nodded in response to her words. "So that makes you more aware of procedure than most of the people who've sat in that chair."

She couldn't tell if he was attempting to extend an olive branch or not. "If you mean do I know that you have to rule me out as a potential suspect before you can move on, yes."

Maybe she wasn't going to give him trouble after all, he thought. The computer sat, ready, its grinding noise reduced to a soft, constant hum. Time to get started.

"No run-ins with—" Tony paused, referring to his notes. The victim's name had momentarily escaped him.

"Rachel," Sasha supplied before he could flip to another page. He raised his eyes to hers. "No, no run-ins. I don't know all that much about her, actually," she warned him. She and the older woman hadn't been friends by any stretch of the imagination, although their paths had crossed a number of times. "Only that she was past retirement age."

The woman had looked it, Tony thought. "Then why didn't she retire?" In his experience, retirement was the carrot people coveted. "She love the job that much?"

Sasha thought of the couple of times she'd overheard the slain nurse complaining about conditions at the hospital, or about a supervisor who was riding her. "I think it was more of a case of her tolerating the job."

"Then why—?" Tony left it to her to fill in the rest.

"The same reason a lot of people stay at a job they don't like. Money. She needed the money," Sasha emphasized. "Rachel had two grandchildren to raise. Her son's sons. Eight and ten I think."

She was making his job easier for him.

He raised his eyes to hers for a second. "Where's the son?" he asked, tapping slowly on the computer keyboard. He typed like someone who had no knowledge of where the letters were arranged.

Sasha shrugged. "Ran off somewhere." She tried to remember what the hospital gossip had been. "I don't think she knew where."

He stopped searching for keys. "So this son took a powder, leaving his kids high and dry, and Rachel stepped in?"

Sasha nodded in response to his question. "According to what I heard, he left the boys with her for the weekend two years ago. Mailed her a letter a month later, said he couldn't handle being a father. Rachel complained about it." To anyone who would listen, she recalled. "But she said she couldn't just let the county raise the boys."

Her words struck a chord. Aunt Tess had said something similar once. Tony shut down the momentary flashback.

Staring at the keyboard, he hunted and pecked in the new information. "Anyone else in the picture?"

He typed so slowly, she had the urge to push him aside and take over. Sasha knotted her hands in her lap. "Her husband. He's a handyman. I think he does work for the apartment complex where they live." She stopped trying to remember bits and pieces and looked at the detective who was engaged in a hopeless duel with the keyboard. "Why are you asking me this? Wouldn't you get more information from PM's Human Resources Department?" They all had forms they'd had to fill out when coming to work for the hospital. PM was extremely careful about who they ultimately hired.

"You're doing just fine." Hitting the period that brought the last sentence to an end, he sat back and regarded her for a second. "For someone who didn't know the victim, you have a lot of information at your disposal."

Was it her imagination, or was that a veiled accusation of some sort? Sasha could feel herself growing defensive. "I pay attention when people talk."

The look he gave her was very pointed. "So do I."

Except, she thought, in his case, what he listened to was probably all related to his work. Detective Santini didn't seem the type to be concerned about people as people, the way she was. Concern was what had brought her into medicine in the first place. It was her overwhelming desire to heal, to fix, to make things right if she could that had made her decide to become a doctor. She'd gone into obstetrics because there she also had the added thrill of seeing new life coming into the world.

It helped balance out the times when she *couldn't* fix things or make them right again.

"A man who listens. Your wife must be a lucky

woman." It was a flippant, sarcastic thing to say, but she was edgy and wired and heartsick all at the same time. She'd forgotten that he'd told her he was widowed.

Santini looked at her sharply. Had she been standing, Sasha thought, she would have reflexively taken a step back, like someone on the receiving end of a physical blow. Obviously, the wound was still very fresh. It wasn't like her to have forgotten something like that, even if he was a stranger. She attributed it to the fact that she was very shaken.

"Sorry," she offered.

His voice was completely dead when he responded. "Nothing to be sorry about."

The silence hung between them, thick, uncomfortable. At least, it felt that way to her. Sasha took another stab at making amends. "I got personal and I shouldn't have. It's a habit I have."

His eyes met hers again. "Talking first and thinking second?" he guessed.

That stung. "Your turn to apologize," Sasha said after a beat.

A small, faint smile played along his lips before retreating. She had guts, he thought again. Brains, beauty and guts. On a good day, she was probably a very dangerous lady to tangle with. "I guess that makes us a couple of sorry people."

She didn't know if he meant it as a joke, but she gave him the benefit of the doubt and smiled anyway.

Tony asked her a few more questions, including inquiring about her immediate whereabouts around the time of the murder and if there was anything further she could tell him about the victim.

She noticed that he used the word *victim* rather than Rachel's name. It made it sound so impersonal, so detached. But, she supposed that was probably a defense mechanism on his part. Otherwise, after all the horrible things he'd undoubtedly encountered as a homicide detective, he would have become completely paralyzed emotionally.

She wasn't completely certain that he wasn't now.

Taking a breath, Sasha told him everything she could remember.

"Rachel didn't stay after hours and socialize," she told him. "At least, not that I know of. She came, did her work, and went home." Rachel never tried to get away with anything, but neither did she feel the need to give more than she was being paid for. She wasn't one to go the extra foot, much less the proverbial mile.

Tony looked thoughtfully at what he'd typed. "Except for tonight."

"Except for tonight," Sasha repeated softly. And then she looked at him as a fresh thought struck her. "Who's going to tell her husband? Who's going to tell Arthur?"

Arthur. That had to be the handyman husband, Tony thought. "I am." He'd done it more times than he cared to remember, and he hated it each and every time, but someone had to and he was not one to shirk responsibilities. He rose from his chair. They were done here for the night. "As soon as I take you home."

She got to her feet as well. "To the hospital," Sasha corrected. "My car's still in the parking structure."

"Okay," he agreed, mentally changing his route, "I'll take you to the hospital. There are still patrolmen there." Dropping her off would be safe.

"Look, why don't you take me to Rachel's place first?" she suggested suddenly. Tony looked at her quizzically. Now what? "This is going to be a huge shock for her husband when you tell him. He's not in the best of health. He had a heart attack just before the children came to live with them. You don't want to chance that happening again." She gave a half shrug. "Maybe I can help soften the blow."

Tony searched her face, looking for signs of logic, trying to understand her reasoning. "How do you do that, Doc? How do you soften death?"

Was he insulting her? Sasha looked at him. "Are you always this abrasive, or do I just bring it out in you?"

He didn't answer. Not directly. "Actually, this is one of my better days."

Sasha rolled her eyes and shook her head. "God help the world."

"My thought exactly." It was a droll remark at his own expense, she thought. Except that he was looking at her when he said it. "Okay, you want to come,

come." She was surprised he didn't offer more of a resistance. "You can help with the kids if they're up."

Sasha walked toward the doorway. "We seem to be on the same page, Detective."

"I wouldn't get used to that if I were you."

She looked at Santini a second before she preceded him into the corridor. "I wouldn't dream of it, Detective."

As it turned out, Rachel's grandsons were not up and neither was her husband. It took a great deal of knocking and ringing before the sound of any sort of rustling was heard from within the first-floor apartment.

Opening the door a crack, leaving the chain securely fastened and in place, Arthur Wells looked like a man who'd been pulled out of the arms of a very deep sleep. His eyes at half-mast, he resisted taking the chain off even after Tony held up his badge for inspection. It was only after he heard Sasha introduce herself and say that this was about his wife that he finally opened the door for them.

"Rachel's mentioned you, Doctor," Arthur told her, gesturing toward his living room. "She worked with you in the ER once," he recalled for her benefit, in case she didn't remember. "Said you were something to watch under pressure. My Rachel doesn't usually give favorable comments." A smile quirked across his lips nervously, as if he was instinctively attempting to forestall something he knew he didn't want to hear. He looked from her to the detective. "Can I get you something?" Arthur began to edge away toward the small kitchen. "Coffee? Water? I've got some soda in the refrigerator, but—"

"Mr. Wells," Tony began, his tone serious, his expression more so.

Frightened, nervous brown eyes darted toward the detective, then toward her, silently imploring her not to allow any words to be said that couldn't be taken back. Words that would ultimately shatter and destroy his small world.

Sasha stepped in between the detective and Mr. Wells. Barefoot, he was shorter than she was, but almost as wide as he was tall. At the moment, he looked completely devoid of strength, as if every one of his years weighed heavily on his shoulders. She took the man's hands in hers. They were large, capable and rough, reminding her of her father's hands. There was nothing that her father couldn't repair or build if he set his mind to it. She had a feeling Arthur was the same way.

Her heart went out to the man. "Mr. Wells," she began softly, "I am very, very sorry—"

"No," he moaned, tears springing to his eyes, "No, no, no."

The burly man began to sway. Sasha threw her arms around him and was just barely able to keep him from sinking to the floor. She looked over her shoulder at the detective. "A little help here."

Tony stepped in quickly, assuming the bulk of the

sagging weight. Between them, they managed to get Arthur to the sofa.

"Not the best bedside technique," Tony commented, stepping back from the man.

Obviously a case of the pot calling the kettle black, she thought. For the sake of the grieving man on the sofa, she bit back a more terse retort and merely replied, "Like you said, there's really no way to soften a blow like this."

Arthur's wide, florid face looked drained. He took two quick breaths to sustain himself before trying to speak.

"Is she—is she—?" But he couldn't bring himself to finish the question, to say the words that would acknowledge his final separation from the wife he'd loved and fought with for forty-three years.

Tony delivered the news swiftly. To him, it was like removing a Band-Aid. You tore it off quickly. Anything else only prolonged the agony. "Someone killed her in the parking garage at PM."

Arthur's eyes widened in confusion. "The parking garage?" he echoed, shaking his head as if there had to be some sort of mistake, some sort of mix-up. "We don't even have a car."

"Then someone must have lured her there," Tony concluded.

Under what pretext? he wondered. Another piece of the puzzle that didn't seem to fit anywhere. *Yet*. And instead of a single murder, or two, it looked as if they had a serial killer on their hands. Targeting nurses? All nurses, or just those from that particular hospital? Or was there something else entirely going on?

"Who? Why?" Arthur cried, his voice cracking with each word.

"That's what we're trying to find out, Mr. Wells," Tony told him. He began to ask the man a question, but Sasha cut him off.

"Do you have anyone we could call for you? Someone who could stay with you?" Sasha asked. She could feel Tony glaring at her, but right now, this was more important, making certain that the man didn't remain alone in the first few hours of his grief.

Arthur looked at her blankly, as if thinking was far too hard a process for him to cope with. And then, just as she was about to repeat the question, he nodded. "Rachel's brother. Her younger brother." The words were tumbling out, disjointed. He was struggling not to cry. "Jerry. I can call Jerry."

Sasha was already taking out her cell phone. "Give me his telephone number, Mr. Wells. I'll call him for you."

Arthur swallowed, nodding his head. It took him a few minutes before he could remember the numbers in the right order. But before she could begin pressing the proper buttons on the cell phone keypad, he caught her wrist.

"Could you stay with me until Jerry gets here?" he asked brokenly. "If the boys wake up—oh God, what am I going to tell the boys?" He looked at her, stricken. "Their father and mother already walked out on them. How are they going to deal with this?"

"Kids are more resilient than you think," Tony told him before she had a chance to reply.

Sasha looked at the tall detective, wondering what he had gone through in his own life that would make him say something like that. He didn't strike her as the kind of man who would offer up empty platitudes in order to comfort anyone. She doubted if he knew how.

"I'll stay with you," she promised, then pressed the keys that connected her to Rachel Wells's brother. She braced herself for the ordeal.

His hands shoved into his pockets, Tony waited until she finished talking to the victim's brother. When she terminated the call, he took her aside.

"Why are you doing this?"

The blunt question caught her off guard. Didn't this man have a clue about what people felt? "Because I hate to see anyone in pain," she said simply. And that was it, the long and the short of it. The sum total of what motivated her.

He glanced over toward Arthur, then back at her. "Look, I can't—"

She anticipated his words. "You don't have to stay here with me. I can catch a cab back to the hospital and get my car after his brother-in-law gets here." She paused for a second, trying to conquer the kernel of fear that threatened to erupt, then asked,

"You've got patrolmen posted there, don't you? I mean, it's still a new crime scene, right?"

"Right."

She was trying to mask it, but she was afraid. Fear was a good thing, it kept civilians from doing reckless things—something he didn't put entirely past her. Tony blew out a breath. He didn't like the idea of her going back to the parking structure alone. His men had swept through all the levels, but there were no guarantees in life about anything.

"Hang on," he finally said. "Let me make a call."

Before she could ask why he was even bothering to mention making a call to her, Tony had turned away, connecting to someone with a single press of a button. With a shrug of her shoulders, Sasha turned her attention to the broken man sitting on the sagging sofa.

He looked, she thought as she came over to him, as if someone had stolen his soul.

Sitting down beside him, she placed her hand over his. "You need to stay strong, Mr. Wells. For your grandsons' sake. They're going to need you more than ever."

"What about me?" Arthur wanted to know, his voice breaking. "What about what I need?"

"That comes later," she said softly. "You do what you have to to get through a day, and then two days and then a week. A month…until there's enough time between you and the pain for you to be able to attempt to handle it."

Arthur shook his head. A tear slid down, hitting the top of her hand. "I don't think I can."

"You can." Her voice was firm beneath the soft tone. "We're all stronger than we think we are."

Numbly, Arthur nodded his head, staring straight ahead at the framed candid shot of his wife on the coffee table. She was laughing. He looked as if he never would again.

Sasha could sense the detective's eyes on her before she looked up to see him standing there. Santini was less than a foot away, looking at her with an expression she couldn't begin to read.

He flipped the phone closed. "I'll stay with you until his brother-in-law comes."

There was no room for selfless protests so she didn't bother making any. She welcomed the company.

Chapter 5

Bart Henderson hung up the phone with such force the resulting contact sounded as if something was being thrown. It caught Tony's attention. He raised an inquiring eyebrow and looked in his partner's direction. Of the two of them, the burly Henderson was the one who could be accused of being sunny, despite the fact that each morning, Tony could overhear him reviewing a litany of complaints about what offending part of his body hurt the most that day. He was usually exchanging the information with the other "old-timer" in the squad room, Harold Lincoln.

Henderson usually didn't display any evidence of a shortness of temper. As far as Tony knew, his partner's temper had no end.

Unlike his own.

Henderson sighed, leaning back in his chair. The resulting breeze ruffled a few papers on his desk, bringing them precariously close to the edge. He moved them back where they belonged and narrowed his small eyes even further. They nearly disappeared beneath the tufts of fading red eyebrows as he looked at his partner.

"That was the hospital administrator at Our Lady of Patience Memorial Hospital. Again," he growled. "She wants to know if we've made any headway in our investigations." The man glanced in his direction hopefully. "Have we?"

Tony thought of the cool, tall blonde he'd interviewed the morning after the first body had been discovered, and then again when the second was found. In her late forties and slender, Lauren James had a chin that seemed to be permanently raised, giving her the appearance of looking down on everyone she dealt with. Her manner did nothing to change that impression.

Tony shook his head. "Not unless there's been a break in the case in the last five minutes that I don't know about."

They'd been at this for three weeks now, fielding calls from well-meaning people that always led nowhere, interviewing everyone remotely associated with the two women and relentlessly going over the data that the crime labs sent up. So far, they were no further along than when they'd started.

"Dunno why she's calling me. You're the one she talked to before." Henderson looked at him over the top of his rimless glasses. "I guess maybe I look friendlier to her."

"Maybe," Tony agreed, already retreating back into the file he'd been reviewing when Henderson had intentionally dropped the receiver.

Restless, Henderson rocked in his chair. "She says the murders are bad publicity for the hospital."

"Murders generally are," Tony commented, trying to block out the annoying sound made by Henderson's chair. Certain sounds had a tendency to distract him.

Just like certain thoughts did. And ever since he'd taken this case, he'd found that doctor, the one who'd been the first one on the scene both times, intruding into his thoughts at very odd, unforeseeable times. He didn't know what to make of it yet.

Maybe his mind trying to tell him something he'd missed. And then again, maybe not.

Tony turned his chair and looked back at the bulletin board on the wall behind him. The actual board had a multitude of tiny holes, evidence of all the thumbtacks that had been driven into it over time, securing bits and pieces of other murders he'd solved. Or that had temporarily been left unsolved.

The puzzles gave him no peace until he either solved them or something larger took their place. But once that was done, once the current case was put to bed, the old, unsolved cases would resurface to haunt him until he finally had all the pieces in the right place. Until he found the killer.

Because of his junkyard-dog tendency never to let go, Tony had an unprecedented record for solved homicides within the precinct. Probably, he'd been told, within the country.

Right now, the board had the photographs of both nurses and every scrap of information he and Henderson had gathered that stood out. The rest of the information existed within his notebook and the hard drive of his computer. A great deal of that overlapped.

There wasn't much to go on. Both victims were females, both were nurses, both worked at PM, but then the similarities ended. The two women had moved in different circles. One had been in her twenties, the other in her sixties, one was a single mother, the other a grandmother raising two grandchildren. They were both struggling to get by, but he didn't see that as a strong connecting factor.

At least, Tony amended, looking from one photograph to the other, not yet.

And what did the note that they'd both been clutching mean? Obviously, it was from the killer. Was it someone who hated nurses in general and wasn't educated enough to know that the phrase he'd typed referred to physicians and not nurses?

Or was it more personal than that? More devious than that? Was there a clue within a clue that he wasn't seeing?

"You know," he theorized out loud, "one of the

murders could have been committed to cover the other."

Henderson pushed away from his desk and turned his chair to face him. "Come again?"

Tony stood up and went to the board. "Someone had it in for either Angela or Rachel and kills the other one to make it look like some dumb serial killer is on the loose."

Henderson wrinkled his brow, trying to follow the reasoning. "Why dumb?"

Tony glanced at the data beneath each photograph, summarizing the last few hours of each victim's life. Nothing remarkable sprang out. "'First do no harm' is the beginning of the Hippocratic Oath, not a pledge a nurse makes."

"Maybe they should have." When Tony looked at his partner, Henderson shrugged his wide shoulders beneath the hound's-tooth jacket he always wore. "Maybe one of them—or both—did some harm."

Tony slowly nodded his head. It was a possibility. But only one of many. It carried no extra weight at the moment.

For the time being, he mentally filed it away.

"Nothing stands out, yet," he told Henderson. And he could only sit at his desk, playing with papers, pecking his way along on the keyboard, for so long. He needed to be hands-on, to be out in the field. "I'm going back to the hospital to nose around. Talk to the security guard who found the first one."

Henderson was already shutting down his machine. "Don't forget that doctor," he said when Tony gave him a quizzical look. "She was around for both murders. Seems like an odd coincidence," he commented affably.

Tony shook his head. "I told you, I've already ruled her out."

Henderson walked down the corridor. A knowing smile moved the ends of his handlebar moustache. "That kind of woman does cloud the mind."

Tony shot the other man an annoyed look. "There's nothing cloudy about my mind. According to the M.E.'s time frame, Dr. Pulaski was five stories away from the scene of both crimes. During the first, she was dealing with a hemorrhaging patient and during the second, she was making her rounds. In each case, a lot of people saw her."

Henderson looked willing to be convinced, but still slightly skeptical. "Making rounds that late in the day?"

Tony's careless shrug indicated that he didn't care what Henderson thought doctors did. He was only interested in one. And only so far as the case went. "Woman's dedicated, I guess."

Reaching the elevator, Henderson pressed the down button. "Nice to know there's someone else out there other than us." And then he laughed. "'Course, she probably makes a hell of a lot more money than either one of us."

Tony laughed shortly. As far as salaries went,

cops were on the low end of the scale. But it had never been about the money for him.

Getting into the elevator, he looked at his partner. "I didn't picture you being in it for the money."

"Not me. I'm strictly in it for the glamour," Henderson deadpanned, then laughed. "And to get material for my book."

The elevator doors closed noisily. A grinding noise accompanied their descent to the ground floor. Henderson had a book? This was the first he'd heard on the subject, Tony thought. But then, he didn't exactly leave himself opened to exchanges that went beyond the cases they were handling.

"What book?"

A faraway look entered Henderson's faded green eyes. "The book I intend to write once I finally retire from this job."

For the first time that morning, Tony smiled. Henderson could no more retire than he could grow another set of arms. This was where he felt he belonged and they were going to have to surgically remove him from his desk to get him to leave permanently.

The elevator came to a stop and the doors drew open. Tony got out. "You keep telling yourself that, Henderson," he tossed over his shoulder. "You keep telling yourself that."

He hadn't planned on revisiting the doctor he'd silently dubbed Snow White. The one Henderson seemed still to be suspicious of. He and Henderson had parted company at the hospital elevators, each intent on their own line of questioning. Henderson had gone to the place where Rachel had reported for the last six months of her life, the surgical floor, while he had gone to the nurses' station on the maternity ward where Angela Rico had worked for over two years.

Had the dark-haired obstetrician not been on the floor, he wouldn't have gone out of his way to see her. But he didn't have to. She was right there.

He'd stopped at the nurses' station where Angela Rico had sat, making notes on patients' charts and talking to the people she worked with. A couple of minutes later, Dr. Sasha Pulaski came walking out of one of the rooms, looking tired and harried.

It was too early in the day to look like that, he thought. But then, maybe the day had come on the heels of a hard night. He supposed that gave them something in common. Both of them could be summoned out of bed at a moment's notice. And there was no saying no once the call came.

Their eyes met as the doctor was passing the nurses' station. Tony rose from what had unofficially been Angela's desk, moving into the corridor. Blocking her way.

"Doctor," he said, nodding at her.

"Detective," she returned. He noticed that the woman drew in her breath, as if she expected him to ask her something.

But just for a split second, as he glanced down at

the button that was coming undone on its own just at the point he assumed was the top of her bra, he'd lost his train of thought. And every other thought as well. But only for a moment.

"Have you thought of anything to add to your statement?" he finally asked.

She'd gone over the events of those two evenings a thousand times in her mind. There was nothing new to add, nothing she'd forgotten to tell him.

Sasha shook her head. "You don't have any suspects?" She knew if he did, he couldn't elaborate, but it was worth a shot. Besides, she was feeling strangely awkward and very aware that the two nurses in the glass-enclosed station were staring at her. At them. And taking in every word that was being said.

"No one who crosses over into both areas," Tony replied after a moment.

They'd found out that Rachel's husband owed a local bookie almost five hundred dollars, but Tony couldn't see his way clear to the bookie killing Arthur's wife because of a payment default, or even as a warning for others. Besides, Angela's background was clean and so was her ex-husband's. Neither was even remotely connected to the bookie so there was no common ground on that score.

Tony's stomach growled, reminding him that breakfast had been half a muffin and lunch hadn't happened for him yet. An impulse struck him and he went with it before he gave it any thought. "You in a hurry?"

Sasha's first reaction was to say yes. As far back as she could remember, she'd always been in a hurry. There was always something to catch up on, something to do.

But at that moment, there was nothing actually pressing that she needed to get to. Her office was located in the medical building across the street and it wouldn't be open again until two o'clock. For once, the waiting room wasn't jammed with patients who'd been forced to restructure their day because she was called away to deliver yet another baby who had no respect for due dates.

Technically, that made her free. "A little less than usual," she told him. "Why?"

Not one to put himself entirely out on a limb all at once, he began with, "Where's a good place to eat around here?"

Humor appealingly curved her mouth. "Believe it or not," she said, knowing what people thought of hospital food, "the food in the cafeteria isn't half bad."

It wasn't the food he was actually interested in. Talking to the doctor in surroundings that put her at ease was his real goal. "I was shooting for three-quarters good."

The smile became a grin. "For that, you'd have to go to Queens."

On his own, he favored takeout, usually from a pizza place. "Why Queens?"

Without making a conscious decision one way or

another, Sasha had begun walking toward the bank of elevators at the rear of the floor. The detective, as she'd expected, had fallen into step with her.

"That's where my parents live," she told him. "My mother's a fantastic cook. Dad keeps telling her she should open her own restaurant, but she doesn't want the hassle or the risk, she tells him."

They stopped at the elevators. Tony glanced at his watch. "Not enough time to go to Queens and back for lunch. Guess I'll have to chance the cafeteria." His eyes held hers for a moment. "Want to be my guide?"

She found it took effort to stop the shiver that threatened to sweep up and down her spine like a runaway roller coaster. She did, however, manage to sound cool as she instructed, "Just take the elevator down to the basement. Can't miss it." And then, as the elevator arrived and its doors opened, she decided to see if she could get anything out of the detective. "On second thought, maybe I could stand to grab something to eat, too."

They got in and he brushed past her to press the button. However minor, the swift, fleeting contact was not lost on either of them. Feeling just the slightest bit awkward, Tony dropped his hand to his side. "I'm sure your patients would appreciate it."

Sasha kept her back to the wall, wishing someone else was on the elevator with them. "My patients?

He nodded. Two people stepped on at the next floor. He moved closer to her. "People think and react better when they eat regular meals."

There was no place for her to back up into. Trapped, she forced herself to sound amused. "You a part-time nutritionist?"

The doors opened again and the two passengers got off. Tony made no effort to step back into his original space. He noticed that she shifted, inching her way to the side. He shook his head in reply. "Something my aunt used to say to us when we wanted to skip meals."

"Us?" She knew nothing about the man and saw this as a chance to give the detective some kind of depth and dimension.

"My brothers and me," he answered. He saw the interest in her eyes. He didn't have long to wait for the next question.

"Your aunt raised you?"

It hadn't been his intention to answer, but somehow the words seemed to flow naturally—even though the memories were jagged and sharp. It hadn't been a warm and fuzzy childhood by any stretch of the imagination. "I wouldn't exactly call it raised. More like stood guard as we grew."

On the second floor, several people got on, all bound for the first. This time, Sasha stepped into his space, her curiosity blocking out any claustrophobic feelings his close proximity might have aroused.

"But you lived with her," she pressed.

He tried to summon the good moments and found them lost amid a sea of bad ones. Still, Tess had done the best she could, he supposed. "Yeah."

The single word said it all, she thought. His had been a hard childhood. Probably had contributed a great deal to the man she saw in front of her today. Unsmiling. Hard. "Because you wanted to or you had to?"

It struck him as an odd way of phrasing the question. He looked at her as they came to the first floor and the same people who'd crowded on, got off. Their places were taken by people who wanted to reach the basement. Now he and the doctor were all but standing in each other's spaces. Not, he noted, an unpleasant thing. But distracting, highly distracting. "I never heard it put that way."

She found herself whispering to him in order not to be overheard or have her words mingling with anyone else's. There were at least three other conversations going on in the small enclosure.

"Is that your way of saying you're not going to answer the question?"

The woman was quick on the uptake, he thought, somewhat amused. "Something like that." He looked down at her. She had to be about five, six inches shorter than him, he guessed. And softer, remembering one feel of her hand. "I'm supposed to be the one asking questions," he pointed out.

The elevator doors opened again and the people in front of them quickly got off. "I thought you were the one who was just going to get some lunch. I didn't realize this was official."

"Off the record," he countered, getting off right beside her.

A long, brightly lit hallway greeted him. Freshly painted arrows pointed in opposite directions, one toward the out-patient pharmacy and the other toward the cafeteria.

Without looking, Sasha turned left. Striding quickly, he fell into step beside her again.

"Off the record or on, it's going to be the same information, Detective. I told you everything I knew, which wasn't much. And if anything had occurred to me, I would have called you." She wove her way in and out of the crowd like someone accustomed to doing this on a regular basis. He did his best to keep up.

"I still have your card," she told him. She carried it around with her every day. Looked at it every night as she emptied her pockets. Looked at it and conjured up an image that unsettled her as it seemed to embed its way beneath her skin.

"Good to know," he allowed. "All right, this is just lunch, then."

"Just lunch," she echoed, making it sound like a pact.

The second Sasha pushed the swinging cafeteria doors open, a wall of noise and increased warmth engulfed them. The cafeteria was filled almost to capacity.

"I guess you were right about the food," he said, lowering his head to her ear so that she could hear him. "Is it always like this?"

His breath cascaded along her neck, making her feel warmer than any of the hospital heating ducts going full blast in the winter. She did her best not to react, not to shiver in the wake of the tingling sensation that was shimmying up and down her spine.

"It's lunchtime," she pointed out. "And a lot of the staff doesn't actually get a full hour. Lauren James has a myriad of rules she wants followed and she doesn't tolerate people bending them."

Picking up a tray, he handed it to Sasha, then took one for himself before following her into the actual food area.

There were two different steam tables offering up four different kinds of entrées, while beds of ice presented a variety of salads and desserts. Tony felt his stomach tightening in anticipation, urging him to make a choice, any choice. It no longer mattered what.

He pointed to a stew and the white-attired server behind the table gingerly placed it on his tray. Tony noted Sasha selected a spinach salad. With a bit of ice still attached to the bottom of the dish, the salad slid around drunkenly on her tray until she brushed the sliver aside.

"Watching your weight, Doctor?" he asked as they both went to the coffee island. Taking the coffeepot, he poured two cups.

"No, I just like spinach." And then she smiled as she paused to pick up an apple that was nestled in another bed of ice shavings. "Me and Popeye."

It was so noisy, he was forced to read her lips in order to hear her. Dr. Sasha Pulaski had the most dazzling smile he ever remembered seeing. Not because her teeth were blindingly white, but there was something sweet and genuine about the smile. Because he was a devout cynic who questioned everything, he couldn't help wondering if the woman behind the smile was putting him on, or if she was as sweet as the smile she displayed.

He also wondered what the chances were of his finding that out before the investigation was over.

"Ring them up together," he instructed the cashier, a thin, sinewy-looking Latino with large, round eyes and an electric blue T-shirt and jeans that adhered to him like a second skin.

Sasha reached into the deep pockets of her lab coat. "I can pay for my own lunch, Detective."

He steadied her hand with his own. "I'm sure you can. Consider this a reward for steering me in the right direction."

"A reward?" she echoed.

Okay, wrong word, he thought. "My way of saying thanks," Tony amended.

She wasn't about to be in his debt for any reason. The ground there was uncertain. "No thanks needed." Sasha began to reach into her pocket again.

"You two want to take this mutual admiration society somewhere else?" the chunky lab technician behind them suggested, annoyed. "You're holding up the line."

"Looks like the public has spoken," Tony told her, placing a twenty into the cashier's hand.

"I'll pick up the next tab," Sasha informed him as she began to scan the area, looking for somewhere to sit.

The word *next* hung in the air, daring him to take it seriously.

Chapter 6

"What can you tell me about Lauren James?"

The question seemed to come out of the blue after several minutes of silence between them had gone by. Tony had sampled the stew and decided that the doctor was right. The food here was more than edible. He'd consumed several more forkfuls before saying anything. Once the hollow feeling had faded from his stomach and he felt a little more human, he felt up to addressing some of the issues that had occurred to him.

Sasha raised her eyes from her salad. "What do you mean?"

He'd always felt that vague questions were the best for openers. That left interpretation up to the person being questioned. A great deal of information could be garnered that way. "What do you know about her?"

But the doctor apparently wanted him to be specific. "You mean her background?"

Tony shook his head. He wasn't after facts he could get from a human resource file. He wanted impressions. "No, I already have that—"

"Of course you do," Sasha murmured, a slanted smile making a brief appearance on her lips. He struck her as someone who left no stone unturned. And if there were no stones, he probably went out and found some.

Santini shrugged casually as he continued eating. "Part of the job."

"I know." Her father had always been thorough like that. She was fairly certain that every boy she and her sisters ever dated had a complete background check conducted on him. "You probably have everybody's background on some tiny little microchip."

"Not everybody's," he corrected, trying to decide if she considered that a job well done, or an invasion of privacy, "just the people who figure directly into the case."

Her eyes met his. "Like me."

That went without saying. "You were on the scene both times."

Sasha popped a cherry tomato into her mouth before commenting. She loved the taste of tomatoes. "Then it must have put you to sleep."

He narrowly avoided being hit on the back of his head by a woman with a large purse that could have doubled as a briefcase. He moved his head away just in time as she hurried on her way.

"What did?" he asked.

"Reading about my background. Nothing remarkable." She recited what she knew had to be in his notes. "I went to NYU for my undergraduate degree, then attended NYU medical school." She didn't add that despite the fact that she worked three nights a week as a waitress to help defray the costs, she still managed to graduate in three years instead of four. "I interned at PM, then was lucky enough to get a residency here and now I can't think of anywhere I'd rather work than here. Like I said, deadly dull." And then she paused. "Or shouldn't I use the word *deadly?*"

"You shouldn't use either word." He would have left it at that, except that she looked at him curiously, waiting for an explanation. "I don't think you're dull."

Her smile made all her features soften and stirred something within him he didn't welcome disturbed. "Then you obviously have a very low excitement threshold, Detective. I live and breathe my work and my family—not always in that order."

Tony knew all about her family. About the parents who had managed to be smuggled out of Krakow, Poland, while that country was still in the grip of communist rule. How Josef and Magda Pulaski had both worked diligently to provide a better way of life for their daughters.

"Four sisters, all younger, all doctors or almost doctors." And then he added the part he knew she didn't expect him to know about. "And each one helps the next in line until that sister graduates. And then it's on to the next one." He paused to take a sip of his coffee. And to use the cup to cover the hint of a smile. "You can close your mouth now."

She inclined her head. The man really was thorough. Or was that because he'd initially regarded her to be a suspect?

"You *have* been doing a lot of research."

He shifted the focus away from himself. "Your parents must be very proud."

Sasha smiled. "They've been known to brag a little," she allowed. Actually, given half a chance, her father bent every ear that came his way about his daughters' accomplishments.

But she had a question of her own for Santini. "If your research is that intense, Detective, what is it you want me to tell you about Lauren James that you don't already know?"

That was easy. He wanted her to tell him what he couldn't find in a report. "What do you think of her?" Before she could answer, he broadened the scope. "What does everyone else think of her?"

Sasha thought of several conversations she'd overheard, usually after Lauren had come down hard on someone. Or fired one of the staff for some minor infraction.

She shook her head. "My father taught me not to

use words like that at the table." And then she smiled. "My mother taught me not to use words like that at all, but my father's way is a compromise." She could see that the detective was still waiting for some kind of an answer. "Nicely put, no one would have the slightest objection if Lauren was hit by a bus as she was crossing the street. She's not exactly a people person when it comes to the staff. Her bottom line is profit."

"I thought that Our Lady of Patience Memorial was supposed to be a non-profit hospital."

She liked the way Santini said the hospital's full name. Liked, she realized, sitting here, having lunch with him. That wasn't really a good thing, Sasha reminded herself. Because "like" led to other things. At this point in her life, she was too busy to get involved with anyone and even if she wasn't, she'd learned her lesson. Being involved meant hurting. Unlike childbirth, this kind of pain was not worth it in the end. Because at the end, there was only heart-ache.

She focused on his question. "It is."

His eyes narrowed as he tried to comprehend the connection between that and what she'd just said about the administrator. "Then I don't understand—"

"There's profit, and then there's profit." *Clear as mud, Sash,* she mocked herself. "Because PM is non-profit, whatever extra money is accumulated over the course of the year is put into updating equip-ment, or the facilities, in order to lure prestigious physicians to affiliate themselves with our hospital. We have a reputation as one of the best hospitals in the state."

Tony read between the lines. "So she's on a power trip."

It was as good a summation as any. She'd already heard one of the nurses refer to Lauren as Stalin in drag, a remark that had particular meaning for her, given her family background.

"Something like that," Sasha agreed. "And there are various ways to gain from being at the helm of a thriving hospital."

"Such as?" he asked with interest. He'd known taking the doctor to lunch was a good idea. That he was having certain warm feelings was, in this case, simply collateral damage.

"Perks that come her way. Things like hard-to-come-by theater tickets and preferential treatment that she wouldn't have gotten if she wasn't the administrative head of Patience Memorial."

Tony frowned. "Isn't that unethical?"

Instead of nodding, Sasha qualified his assumption. "If you get caught."

He wasn't given to winking and looking the other way. But neither was he ready to condemn on hearsay. "These are pretty serious allegations."

Sasha knew what he was thinking, could see it in his eyes. One woman out to destroy the reputation of another. That hadn't been her intent.

"I'm not being catty, Detective. A few things have

come to light recently and several members of the board are looking into the matter. If they don't like the answers they come up with, Lauren might be in for a very rude awakening soon."

"They'd fire her?"

"In a heartbeat."

"Does she know?" If she did, he thought, that might be motive enough to do something drastic. Like damaging the reputation of the hospital that was threatening to put her out. Lauren James didn't strike him as a woman who agonized over her conscience.

Lauren didn't behave as if she knew, Sasha thought. The woman was certainly not going out of her way to make any allies or mend any fences. Still, she was too bright not to know that something was going on. "She might suspect." Sasha saw a look enter his eyes. "Why?" she wanted to know. "What are you thinking?"

"That I need to have another talk with Ms. James."

Sasha second-guessed him. She shook her head. "She's not your killer."

Tony banked down his amusement. Everyone was an armchair detective these days, he thought. "What makes you say that?"

"Because the sight of blood makes Lauren immensely queasy. I once had to give her several stitches because she cut her hand on a broken vase. Lauren passed out before I could prick her skin."

The story aroused his curiosity. "I thought you dealt mainly with, um, the other end," he finally said politely.

"I happened to be in her office when she cut her hand." She had never believed in standing on the sidelines when she could help. She hadn't been raised that way. "Seemed like the thing to do at the time."

He nodded, but he had already made up his mind. For all he knew, the murders had been committed to embarrass the administrator. Sideways thinking was the norm rather than the exception. "I'm still going to have another talk with her. In this job, you never know when a stray comment might lead to something that solves the case."

She would imagine that there were an incredible amount of pieces for him to consider and sift through. Sasha finished her coffee and set down the cup. "Your head must ache from all those pieces that you're trying to fit together."

"I manage." His tone gave nothing away as he watched her eyes, wondering where, if anywhere, she was going with this.

She trod lightly, but as a doctor, she felt obligated to point out certain things. "Drinking only intensifies headaches."

Tony looked at her, surprised at her comment. Surprised, too, that she should feel free to make it. Because the job had kept him on the move these last three weeks, there hadn't been any extra time to dwell on the black hole in his personal life that was eating him up alive. Because he was disciplined, he made sure he was always sober while working. He hadn't taken a drink in three weeks.

"What makes you mention drinking?" he wanted to know. There was an edge to his voice.

Her father had warned her more than once that she was too fearless. That she didn't allow conventions to hold her back. "That first night, you were hungover."

He drank vodka for a reason. Vodka left no telltale scent to give him away. And he prided himself on being able to navigate like a lifetime teetotaler. But he hated lies and stayed clear of them whenever possible. So he didn't bother pretending that she was imagining things.

Maybe he even had something to learn here. "So, what gave me away?"

It wasn't his behavior. It was more instinct on her part. "There was something in your eyes. Something not quite in sync."

Okay, he'd give her that, although he was pretty certain that he kept a lid on his thoughts and what little there was left of his emotions.

"Didn't have to be alcohol," he pointed out.

"No, it didn't," she agreed. "But whatever had you out of sync, you were trying to block it out with alcohol."

He regarded her for a long moment. "Lady, you're beginning to spook me." He didn't believe in clair-voyants, but he was willing to concede that there were people who were more intuitive than others. "Maybe you should be working on our side."

"I am on your side," she told him quietly. And then, because she felt she needed to explain what had given her insight into his situation, she said, "My fiancé had a cousin who tried to drown his sorrows with more than his share of Scotch. The result was the same. The sorrows didn't go away, but he very nearly did."

Tony had heard only one thing. "Your fiancé?" The background check he'd conducted made no mention of her having anyone in her life who wasn't directly related to her by blood. He glanced at her left hand. There was no ring there, but that didn't necessarily mean anything. "You're engaged?"

Sasha caught her lower lip between her teeth. Damn, how had that slipped out? Maybe because she still felt, even though he was gone, that Adam was still part of her life. "I was."

Was. He had no idea why the tension in his neck seemed to lessen. It was best not to go to places like that. "What happened? He have trouble competing with your career?"

"He had trouble competing with a mugger's gun," she corrected him quietly. She saw mild surprise flicker across the detective's face. Well, she'd come this far, she might as well tell him the rest of it. "Adam was killed trying to keep the man from stealing my engagement ring." She couldn't bring herself to look at it after he'd died so she sold it and donated the money to Adam's favorite charity, where it could do some good. "It was in a parking structure very similar to the one at PM," she added.

Tony took in the information, not knowing what to say, other than, "I'm sorry."

She tried to force a faint smile of gratitude to her lips and failed. "Me, too."

He understood now why she'd looked so shaken, so pale when he'd first met her. As a doctor, she was accustomed to blood, to life and occasionally, to death. But if the scene brought back personal memories, that was a completely different story.

Tony watched her push away her salad. There was still some left in the bowl. "I've made you lose your appetite."

She detected a note of self-reproach and was quick to absolve him of any guilt. "The spinach wasn't all that fresh."

He studied her face for a long moment. "You know, I'm not sure if, as an OB-GYN you'd know this, but if you lie, your nose grows."

The man had a sense of humor after all, she thought. It made her relax a little. Sasha raised her chin. "And is it?"

He looked so serious when he cocked his head, studying her, that for a moment she thought he was actually trying to verify whether her nose was growing.

"Hard to tell in this light," he finally said. She laughed and he nodded his approval. "That's better." Debating, he allowed himself to relate to her on a personal plateau, eschewing the danger of that. "I didn't mean to drag up any bad memories."

"You didn't." This time, she did smile. "All my memories of Adam are good ones."

He understood what she meant. That was the way he felt about his wife. There was a song she'd loved, "It Had To Be You," an old number from the thirties or so. One of the lyrics in it seemed to fit. "And even be glad, just to be sad, thinking of you." There were days that thoughts of Annie were the only things that kept him going.

He saw the doctor drop her napkin on the tray and then rise. She picked up the tray, ready to clear it away. "I'd better be getting back to my office," she told him. "Thank you for lunch."

"I enjoyed the company."

Tony hardly remembered rising to his feet, his own tray in his hand. He hadn't expected to say that when he'd opened his mouth. He'd expected to hear himself say something innocuous, like "you're welcome," or "maybe I'll see you." This was much too personal and revealing.

After a beat, Sasha nodded. The small smile widened just a touch. "So did I."

Whatever else she might have said was interrupted by the insistent buzz emitted by his pager. With a sigh, Tony placed his tray back on the table and reached for the device clipped to his belt. He barely had to glance at it. The number on the screen was all too familiar.

Sasha didn't know whether to linger, or take the

opportunity to drop off her tray on the conveyor belt and leave. Quickly. She didn't like what she was feeling. Attraction. It was crackling between them whenever she was near the detective. She wanted no crackling, no curiosity, no nothing.

She wanted dullness. The dullness that did not interfere with the rest of her life.

Whatever arguments she used on herself, she was still hanging back, watching him take out his cell phone and press a button that connected him to whoever was paging him.

She listened, thinking that perhaps it had something to do with finding Angela and Rachel's killer. Telling herself that it had nothing to do with gathering a few extra moments in the detective's company.

Sasha placed her tray next to his and began to combine the two, moving the plates and utensils onto one tray, then stacking it on top of the other. It bought her a few seconds. Long enough to hear him say, "This is Santini," into the cell phone.

The voice on the other end was male, but that was about all she could distinguish. The words were not clear enough for her to hear.

"You'd better get up here, partner," Henderson said to him.

"Where's 'here'?" Tony wanted to know.

He heard Henderson sigh. "Seventh floor." He paused, as if for dramatic effect. "One of the cleaning crew just found an orderly."

"And?" Tony pressed, waiting for the rest of it.

Out of the corner of his eye, he saw that the doctor was still there and that she was obviously listening to his side of the conversation. Annoyance would have been his usual response, but he found he didn't feel any.

"And the orderly was stuffed into the supply closet at the time. Tony, the guy had a hole in his forehead and the same note in his hand."

Adrenaline shot through Tony's veins. This just kept getting better and better. "Secure the area," he told Henderson.

"Already done. I was going to call for backup, but I thought you'd want me to call you first."

"You thought right, Henderson. Now call for backup." Tony closed his phone. The doctor was still watching his every move, the trays still in her hands.

"Back up, why back up?" she asked the moment he ended the call. "Did your partner find a suspect?"

His expression was sober. "No, just another body."

She stared at him, her eyes widening in horror. This was a nightmare, Sasha thought. The halls of PM were being stalked by a serial killer. "Another nurse?"

He shook his head. "Not this time. Henderson said it was an orderly."

"An orderly?" she echoed. This was making less and less sense. Now it looked as if someone had it in for the hospital. Sasha suddenly realized that

Santini was walking away from her. "I'm coming with you," she called, hurrying after him.

Sasha paused only long enough to throw the combined trays onto the conveyor belt, then she quickened her pace to catch up to him.

Tony held one of the swinging doors open for her. "I thought you had patients to see."

She darted across the threshold. "Not until two o'clock. I was going to catch up on dictation," she told him. "But there's nothing there that won't keep." Her hand covered her own pager, praying that no baby would suddenly decide to come out and see the world in the next forty minutes.

He gave her a glance that would have frozen others in mid-step. It had no such effect on the doctor.

"This isn't exactly according to the rules," Tony said tersely as they strode up the corridor to the elevators.

"Neither is death," she answered quietly, afraid that her voice might carry. There was no telling who might be turning the corner and overhear her.

She had him there, Tony thought. He supposed it would do no harm to let her come along.

The irony of the phrase he'd just used wasn't lost on him. But maybe the doctor knew the victim and could give him a jump-start on gathering information. So far, she seemed to know everyone who worked here.

He wondered, as they rode up the elevator, since

he'd already decided to talk to the administrator if it would be worth his while to corner Lauren James about this latest development. He and Henderson were going to have to start looking into recently terminated, disgruntled employees.

Most of all, he wondered, as he glanced in her direction, why he was really letting the doctor talk her way into coming along.

Chapter 7

Jorge Lopez was a slight man. In his late twenties and a former gang member with an arrest record, the diminutive orderly was finally getting his life together and headed in the proper direction. His job at Patience Memorial was only one of two he held down while going to school at night in order to get his G.E.D. He wanted, he'd confided to the pretty social worker he'd just begun seeing, to make something of himself.

And now, Sasha thought, heartsick as she looked at the prone body that had been discovered less than half an hour ago in the supply room, Jorge was never going to get the chance.

Tony'd examined the orderly's body as best he

could, mindful not to disturb anything until after the crime scene investigators had had a chance to photograph everything and process the scene. There really wasn't all that much to see. There was the note he'd seen on the previous two victims. Like the others, Lopez had been killed with a single bullet to the center of his forehead. Death had been instant. From all indications, a silencer had been used. That would explain why no one had heard the shot.

But not why no one noticed. The body was still warm. That meant that the murder had taken place in the last hour. This was the post-surgical floor. How had the killer escaped notice?

Perturbed, Tony rose to his feet. He exchanged places with a young woman from the crime scene unit. She was armed with a camera and immediately began taking photographs.

"I want their lives gone over with a fine tooth comb," he told Henderson as he stepped back. "The two nurses and the orderly. Everything they had in common. Where they shopped, who they saw. Any clubs they might have liked attending. Hobbies, vices. Anything," he emphasized. There had to be something more going on than just working at Patience Memorial, he thought.

Henderson pursed his lips, looking at the small, dark-haired man on the floor.

"What?" He knew the signs. Henderson was chewing on something.

"This could have been gang payback for something and they're just using the other two murders for cover," Henderson theorized, eyeing him carefully for his reaction.

Tony scrubbed his hand over his face. The thought had crossed his mind as well the second he'd found out about Lopez's former gang affiliation. "Yeah, I know. But for right now, let's just think of Lopez as belonging to this very exclusive little club. I want to make sure we shut the doors before any more members walk through them."

Stumped, frustrated, Tony turned to see that the doctor was still standing behind him. She hadn't said a word since they'd approached the supply closet and had actually listened to him when he'd told her to keep to the sidelines. There was pity in her eyes as she looked at the dead man.

Tony walked over to her. "You knew him?"

Sasha continued looking at the crumpled figure on the floor. Surprise was frozen on the handsome face. It all seemed so surreal, so bizarre to her. She'd seen more than her share of dead people when she'd done a rotation in the emergency room during her residency. Like everyone else at the hospital, she'd experienced the unnatural scenario of having a person talk to her one moment, then lapse into a deadly silence as their heart stopped beating the next. But she hadn't actually *known* any of those people, not for more than a few minutes.

She *knew* Jorge.

What was going on in the hospital was far more

personal. This was happening where she worked, where she *lived* a good portion of her life. She felt an overwhelming sadness. More than that, she felt indignant, because she felt violated.

"He was always whistling," she finally said in response to Santini's question. "Not those reedy-sounding efforts you always hear where people sound as if they were blowing out cracker bits. I could hear springtime in his whistle." She raised her eyes, aware that the detective was looking at her. "Jorge seemed very happy, like he didn't have a care in the world. But he did care," she added quickly. "He cared about his work, cared about the patients. Said that maybe in time, he'd become a nurse himself."

And then she smiled as she remembered. "He was always hanging around the OR, ready to do anything in order to be part of what went on in there, even if it was just cleaning up." She turned to look at the detective. "Why would somebody do this?" The question wasn't really directed at him, but at whatever power could supply some sort of half acceptable answer. It just didn't seem fair.

"That," Tony told her, "is the sixty-four-million-dollar question."

He looked thoughtfully down at the slain orderly. The blonde from the crime scene unit had finished taking photographs and was now lifting something from the man's shirt with tweezers. She placed it in a small plastic bag.

Tony slanted a glance at the woman next to him. "Lopez wanted to be a nurse?" He saw the doctor nod in response. "Maybe this nut job has it in for nurses," he theorized. But that didn't explain everything, either. "But if that's the case, what's this bit with the note?" he wondered out loud for the umpteenth time.

Tony was beginning to believe that the victims weren't just picked at random, or murdered in order to get back at the hospital. His gut told him that they were chosen for a reason. Whoever was doing this was too methodical to select just anyone. The killer seemed to know everyone's schedule. How else could he kill his quarry without being seen?

Which meant that it was an insider, he concluded. That narrowed it down to roughly four and a half thousand people, give or take.

"Maybe that's the key," Sasha guessed, still working with what the detective had just said. "Maybe whoever's doing this is trying to make a point, teach a lesson." She looked at the bullet hole in Jorge's forehead. "He's not just shooting them, he's executing them."

Tony raised an eyebrow. "Your father bring his cases home?"

A fond smile curved her mouth. "Sometimes. Not so Mama would see, but late at night, when she was asleep, he'd get up and sneak into the kitchen and spread his notes out on the table. Sometimes he'd sit there for two, three hours, trying to find something he'd missed."

It wasn't anything he hadn't done himself. More than a few times. "And you know this how?"

"I used to hear him and get up, too. Sometimes he'd tell me about the case." Usually after she'd begged and pleaded, she recalled. "I'm sure he kept the gorier details to himself, but he always told me enough to get me caught up in it, make me want to help him."

That would explain why she asked him so many questions, Tony thought. He stepped out of the way as the Medical Examiner arrived. Older, slightly overweight, the nature of his work had left C. S. Vaughn with a perpetual frown on his face.

Without thinking, Tony slipped his hand around Sasha's waist, moving her out of the way as well. Realizing that he was touching her, he dropped his hand. "So why didn't you become a cop like your old man?"

For a while, she'd considered it. But then she'd changed her mind. "I was more interested in life than in death. Besides, both my parents had their heart set on having a doctor in the family."

In light of what he'd learned, the comment made him laugh. "I guess that's a case of careful what you wish for. All that money for medical school," he elaborated when she looked at him quizzically. The cost of putting five daughters through college, let alone medical school, had to be staggering.

"We all pitch in," she reminded him. Education, her father had maintained, was a privilege, not a right. None of them ever forgot that.

Tony was nodding when it suddenly occurred to

him that he'd gotten distracted and veered from the case.

First time that had *ever* happened. He upbraided himself for being so careless.

Looking over his shoulder, he was relieved to see that Henderson was busy talking to the head nurse and hadn't noticed his lapse.

Still, that didn't make it any less of a transgression in his own book, Tony thought, annoyed.

He looked back at the doctor. "You work with this Lopez?"

Lopez. The detective made it sound so impersonal, she thought. Jorge Lopez was a person, not simply a statistic. It was important to her that Santini think of him that way.

"Everyone worked with Jorge," she told him. "His supervisor would send Jorge anywhere he was needed. The man worked twice as hard as anyone else. It was as if he was trying to make up for lost time."

And now he didn't have any time left, she thought sadly.

Santini was writing down everything she was saying in the small notepad she saw him carrying with him. "He have a family?"

She thought a minute, trying to remember. "He has a daughter with an ex-girlfriend. Monica. She's almost six. And I think he'd started seeing someone recently." Her memory became clearer and she nodded. "He showed me her picture. She's a social worker. He thought she could have been a model."

She could remember the man beaming as he showed off the photograph.

The woman had a good head for detail, Tony thought. It made his job easier. "Do you know her name?"

If Jorge had mentioned it, she couldn't remember. Sasha shook her head. "I'll ask around."

Ordinarily he would have told her that they could handle it, but in this case, to varying degrees, she seemed to be interwoven in all three victims' lives and because she was a hospital insider, he decided it was prudent to accept the doctor's offer.

"Thanks." Tony made another notation in his notepad, then flipped it closed for the time being. He tucked it away. "I'll get in touch with you later," he told her.

Tony stopped to confer with the crime scene investigator. When he turned around a couple of minutes later, the doctor was gone. And he was relieved.

With her gone, he hoped his mind would clear.

"We're going to need more manpower," he said to Henderson when the latter crossed over to him several minutes later.

"I was just about to suggest that." The wealth of data to be sorted through was increasing exponentially. It could easily overwhelm them. "Think the captain'll go for it?"

"He'll have to." Tony frowned. There was no doubt in his mind what they were facing. "Any way you slice it, we've got ourselves a genuine, dyed-in-the-wool serial killer on our hands. That means putting together a task force."

And quickly, he added silently. Before anyone else was murdered.

If there was any doubt that a serial killer was loose, the next day's edition of the *New York Daily News* vanquished it. The headline on the front page screamed Death Stalks Patience Memorial.

The second Sasha picked up the paper from her doorstep, the telephone began to ring. She was alone in the apartment. Natalya had pulled an all-nighter and was still at the hospital while Kady had left half an hour ago, saying only that she was off to see a friend.

For a moment, Sasha thought of pouring herself a bowl of cornflakes and ignoring the phone, but that lasted for only one ring. She knew who it was. Ignoring him wasn't going to make him go away.

Getting up from the kitchen table, she crossed to the telephone. One glance at the caller ID told her she was right.

"Hi, Daddy," she said, placing the receiver against her ear.

"How you know that's me?" the deep, heavily accented voice wanted to know as it rumbled in her ear.

Her father had the *Daily News* delivered and read it religiously at breakfast every morning. He'd always been an early riser. She smiled to herself as she brought the wireless receiver back to the table and sat down.

"I've known you for thirty years, Daddy. I pick things up."

Josef didn't waste time beating around the bush. He never did where his girls were concerned. "What is this serial killer thing at the hospital that I am reading about?"

She gave him a thumbnail sketch, although she knew he was asking for more. "Two nurses were killed in the parking structure at PM, and yesterday they found an orderly in the supply closet. He'd been shot like the first two victims."

She heard an impatient breath escape before he said, "I know. I can read, Sasha." Concern throbbed in every syllable. "Do you know anything about these murders?"

"Probably no more than you, Dad." Given his nature and background with the police, she imagined that her father had probably devoured all the stories about the murders. Since he'd retired, time was now a commodity that hung heavily on his hands. The model kits he'd collected for the day he would retire held no interest for him once he was free to devote himself to their construction. So he read mysteries and got himself involved in his daughters' lives. For his own good, and theirs, Sasha wished he'd do more of the first and less of the second.

"They have found nothing?" he asked incredulously. Not waiting for her answer, he said, "Maybe I should call Larry."

Larry was Larry Collins, the chief of detectives. He was a man who had swiftly risen through the ranks, but to her father he would always be the wet-behind-the-ears kid he had been partnered with. The two families got together every Christmas, at which time her father and Larry would sit by the fireplace, talking over cases that had happened "back in the day." She'd treated his wife on a number of occasions at the hospital.

That not withstanding, she didn't think that the chief of detectives would appreciate her father butting in when it came to official police business.

"I don't like you working there, Sasha," he told her. "With a crazy person loose."

She laughed. That was definitely not a reason to change hospitals. "This is New York, Dad. There're a lot of crazy people loose."

Sasha could almost see him scowling, his eyebrows drawing together, creating a formidable line above his hawk-like nose. He could look scary when he wanted to. But she knew that beneath it all was a soft marshmallow center.

"But they are not killing people," her father growled at her. The more he worried, the grumpier he tended to sound.

"That we know of," she pointed out, deliberately keeping her voice cheerful.

There was silence on the other end. Her father was accustomed to these verbal sparring matches. Accustomed, too, to her stubbornness. "Cannot you and your sisters go on a vacation?"

"No," she answered pointedly with feeling. "Daddy, the police are on it. The detective handling the case seems very competent and I'm sure—"

"You have met him?" he wanted to know, interrupting her.

"Yes." She realized that she was smiling and deliberately dropped the corners of her mouth. "He questioned me."

"Questioned you?" her father echoed, indignation rising in his voice. "Why for he question you?" And then he answered his own question, but not to his satisfaction. "He is thinking you are a suspect?"

"Daddy, you know that they have to rule people out before they can get on with the case—"

"But why you?" he pressed. He knew police procedure like the back of his hand. And he missed it more than he would ever tell anyone. "They are not talking to everyone at the hospital." And then it hit him. And he didn't like it. "Did you see something?"

"No." But that was only in the third case, she reminded herself. She'd always believed in being honest whenever possible. So with a resigned sigh, because she knew the kind of reaction to expect, she added, "But I called the police about the first two bodies."

"You?"

Josef tended to be protective of his own and in his eyes, she and her sisters would always be his little girls, in need of caring. She supposed, given a choice between having it this way and having a distant parent who remained uninvolved in her life, she would have chosen the former.

But that still didn't mean she wanted to be smothered. "Dad, please don't worry—"

"Too late," he informed her glibly. "You have children, you worry. God makes it work that way." The sigh she heard told her he was struggling to keep himself in check. "But I thought you would be safe in the hospital."

"I am safe at the hospital," she insisted.

"With a madman loose, killing everyone?" He laughed shortly.

She tried her best to reason with him as her cornflakes gradually became soggier, their wavy shapes being dragged down into the milk.

"Daddy, you're overreacting. He's not killing everyone. Three people have died. Three people too many," she quickly qualified, "but three people do not make an 'everyone' by any stretch of the imagination."

There was silence on the other end. For a second, she thought she'd won. She should have known better. "You know all the people?"

"You mean the people who were killed?"

"Yes."

"Yes," she replied, wondering if she was headed for another minefield, "I know them."

"How?" her father pressed. "From seeing, or from working?"

She was about to say that she knew the three victims from interacting with them on occasion, but then she paused to consider his question more carefully. Angela had been present for several of the babies she'd delivered, but off-hand, she couldn't recall ever having worked with Rachel. As for Jorge, he might have been in the delivery room after the fact, but she was positive he'd never been there during a delivery.

"Seeing, mostly," she finally told him.

"You know, your mother, she says I am making her crazy, hanging around, watching her. I think I am helping and she is saying I am not."

The information had come out of left field. But she knew her father well enough to know that he was not just meandering through a conversation. Everything he said had a reason behind it.

"Where's this going, Daddy?"

"I am thinking," he stretched out slowly, as if to give the impression of thoughts forming, "maybe I could become a security guard. Your hospital, it needs more guards now, yes?"

Oh God, no. That was all she needed, her father following her around as she made her rounds, saw her patients. She knew he meant well, but that didn't change the fact that she didn't want him shadowing her every move.

"Daddy, it's a lovely gesture, but really, I'm fine." And then, before he could say anything, she added, "Natalya's fine. Kady's fine."

"Those nurses and that orderly," he said gruffly, "they were not so fine."

"No," she admitted, "they weren't." This was a grisly matter and she couldn't escape that. But she couldn't let it hinder her, either. "Look, Dad, if you want to be a security guard, I think that's great. But you know it's never a good idea to be personally involved." And if he worked at PM, he would be very personally involved.

"If I am not involved, I can't be doing my work," he told her simply and she knew it was true. While others maintained their sanity by separating themselves from the events of the crimes they were working on, Josef Pulaski dove in and immersed himself in the details and the situation until, on some level, he lived and breathed his work. Caring was his key when it came to solving cases. Caring defined the man.

"You do what you think is best, Daddy," she finally said. "But I am not," she warned quickly, "wearing a bulletproof vest to the hospital."

She heard him chuckle. "You were always a step ahead of me."

Sasha sincerely doubted that, but it was nice to hear.

"Gotta go, Dad."

"I will see you later."

That, Sasha thought, hanging up, was what she was kind of afraid of.

Chapter 8

He couldn't catch a break.

Pulling his chair in closer to his desk, Tony suppressed an exasperated sigh. His back ached and his nerves were frayed and getting more so as he struggled to tune out the noise around him.

For the last hour, he'd been staring at the same files he'd already gone over so many times in the last few weeks, he could recite what was on each page verbatim without bothering to look.

Two weeks had gone by since the last murder. That made it a total of five weeks and nothing. No headway, no ground gained. Theories about the murders still flew around from every direction, to be discounted or placed on a list of possibilities. But five weeks after Angela Rico was first discovered on the lower level of the hospital parking structure, they were no closer to finding her killer or the killer of the other two victims than they had been when the security guard had first stumbled across her body.

Surrounded by a stack of files, Tony drummed his fingers on his desk, an outward sign of the impatience festering beneath the surface.

Each murder was the same. A single bullet to the head. An execution. Each victim had the same note clutched in his or her hand. A note that could have come from any one of a thousand printers located in the general vicinity. There were no prints on the paper other than the victim's. The only trace of a stray fiber found on any of the three bodies had come from the first victim. A single, almost imperceptible blue thread that the lab technician ascertained had come from a uniform. The kind that the security guards at Patience Memorial wore.

That brought their attention momentarily back to the initial security guard. But all it took was a simple re-questioning. Walter Stevens told Henderson that he'd bent over the body, hoping against hope, to see if the slain woman had the slightest pulse still beating.

Tony heard a squeak that seemed amplified above the rest of the noise. He glanced over in Henderson's direction. His partner was leaning back in his chair as far as it would go.

As if sensing that he had eyes on him, Henderson looked in his direction. "It's like he vacuumed and scrubbed the victim and the crime scene before he left."

There was no doubt that these murders were completely premeditated. Those were the hardest criminals to deal with, the ones who operated with no soul, who conducted their crimes with cold logic instead of being driven by heated passion. On some distant, vague level, the latter could be remotely forgivable, the former could not.

Tony tossed down the pen he'd just picked up. "This is one hell of a sick, methodical bastard," he declared.

Raising his eyes, he looked around the office, trying to clear his mind and focus on something, anything that might trigger an original thought about the case. A thought that might take him a little further than this blank wall he found himself mentally staring at.

The captain had finally been persuaded to authorize extra manpower and the extra hours that were needed to search for the Hospital Stalker, as the local papers had dubbed their killer.

Along with the task force and the publicity came the cranks. The phones rang constantly with people calling to offer information that, at this point, either proved useless or was entirely a figment of the caller's imagination. They had also started getting confessions. There were eight so far, all of which had fallen apart when further pursued.

It never ceased to amaze him how deranged and

lonely some people were that they would actually make up something like committing a murder just to garner attention, even if only for a few moments. Some things, he decided, were just outside his frame of reference, even though he knew firsthand what it meant to be so lonely. Didn't matter how lonely someone got, claiming to be a serial killer just didn't sound like a cure for the blues.

This was why the piece of information about the note found clutched in all the victims' hands had deliberately been omitted from all the news releases. The captain had insisted that Lauren James refrain from saying anything as well. The hospital administrator ate up the spotlight like a thirsty flower drew in rainwater, but she had reluctantly agreed. It was the department's only way of verifying whether or not their killer was making a legitimate full confession.

So far, none of the people who had called, confessing, could have possibly committed any of the murders, let alone all three. There were enough holes in their so-called confessions to drive a Mack truck sideways through them.

The restlessness that was so much a part of his life was beginning to surface again. Tony hated being cooped up indoors for any length of time. He supposed it came from having spent so much of his childhood confined to a corner of the small bedroom that he shared with his brothers, always for some minor infraction of Aunt Tess's rules.

"I'm going back to recanvas the hospital," Tony said abruptly as he pushed his chair away from his desk.

"Going to talk to that lady doctor again?" Henderson wanted to know.

Tony glanced in his direction.

Actually, that *was* his intent, to find the doctor again and see if she'd heard anything new herself. She had two sisters associated with the hospital and from the way she conducted herself, he was willing to bet that she was friendly with a good portion of the staff. People would be more likely to tell her things than they would a police detective.

But all he was willing to say to Henderson was, "She's part of the case," with his usual degree of carelessness. Then his eyes narrowed ever so slightly. "Why?"

Henderson's expression was affable. "No reason, just wondering." And then he added with a broad smile, "Mighty pretty lady."

Slipping on his black leather jacket, Tony shrugged off the observation. "Yeah, maybe."

The look on Henderson's face said he wasn't buying into his display of disinterest. "No maybe about it. If I were your age…" Henderson deliberately let his voice trail off.

Tony left the jacket unzipped for the time being. "You'd have another partner because I'd still be in grammar school."

Henderson leaned back in his chair in order to

continue watching him as he walked toward the doorway. "I'm not that old."

"Yeah, you are," Tony tossed over his shoulder.

"Be sure to say hello for me," Henderson called after him.

Tony raised his hand above his head and waved away the words without even turning around.

He didn't see why, after all this time, Henderson had suddenly decided to butt into his business. Maybe, Tony mused as he decided to take the stairs instead of the elevator, that was because until now there hadn't seemed to be any business to butt into.

There still wasn't, he told himself. The sound of his shoes hitting the metal steps followed him down the stairwell.

Leaving his vehicle parked in one of the spaces in the small parking lot that was directly adjacent to PM's emergency room, Tony was just about to cross the hospital's threshold when he was knocked off his feet. A disheveled-looking man in his early twenties came flying through the double glass doors just as Tony was about to enter the building.

Reflexes that had been finely honed on the job, not to mention the neighborhood where he'd grown up, had Tony grabbing the man by the leg and bringing him down before he could make good on his getaway. But not before the man had somehow managed to twist around and slash him with the knife he had clutched in one hand.

The soft black leather he was wearing was the first casualty, the arm beneath it was the second. Tony held on tighter, pinning the fugitive to the ground.

The assailant cursed his luck, the hospital and him. Within less than a minute, the security guards who'd been chasing the man caught up to their quarry.

"Thanks, mister," the tall, blond-haired guard who was first on the scene said. Grabbing the runner's arm, the security guard took possession of his quarry. Smaller, with a slighter build, the fugitive hadn't a prayer of getting away.

"Detective," Tony corrected. Refusing the hand the other, older guard extended to him, Tony rose to his feet on his own power, doing his best not to wince. He tightened his fingers around his left arm. Blood still managed to ooze through the barrier.

"Hey, you'd better have that looked at," the older guard said, concerned.

Tony bit back the urge to point out that the advice was unnecessary. He had no intention of just letting his wound bleed indefinitely. But for the moment, he was more interested in the man whose escape he'd just foiled.

Ordinarily, his first thought might have been that this was the killer they were looking for. But something told Tony as he quickly assessed his assailant that though the man looked somewhat deranged, he didn't look clever enough to be able to cover his bases. And whatever else the killer might be, there was no denying that the man was clever.

Tony nodded at the cursing captive the blond guard was holding onto. "What's he done?"

"Stole some drugs from the supply room," the younger guard said to him with a look of disgust on his face. "Somebody forgot to lock it."

"What floor?" Tony wanted to know. Maybe that somebody had deliberately left the supply room's door unlocked in preparation for another execution. After all, the first two had been in the parking garage, maybe the next two were supposed to be in the same kind of location as well. It would be a sign of an obsessive-compulsive inclination. Tony had learned long ago never to rule anything out, just in case.

"Fifth," the older guard told him. "We got the call from a Dr. Pul-something-or-other."

"Pulaski?" Tony supplied. Fifth floor. That was the maternity floor, he remembered. Where the doctor made her rounds.

The other man smiled, not attempting to repeat the name. "Yeah, that's it."

And that's her, Tony thought, as he saw the woman suddenly burst into the other end of the corridor located outside the emergency room.

His eyes on her, Tony took out his cell phone and called the precinct. With an economy of words, he identified himself, reported the incident and requested that a patrolman be sent out immediately to take the suspect to jail.

He'd just pushed the end-call button when the doctor reached him. She had obviously been running longer than the length of the corridor. There was something very captivating about watching the rise and fall of her chest as she tried to regulate her breathing.

And it bothered him that he enjoyed the view.

Sasha had just finished looking in on her newest patient. Carol Smith was an eighteen-year-old unmarried first-time mom who would have had her baby in an alley if Sasha hadn't spotted her less than an hour ago. She'd brought the girl into the hospital just as her contractions were coming less than two minutes apart.

Carol had no insurance, but PM never turned anyone away. The patients who ultimately couldn't pay their hospital bills provided PM with their tax write-offs at the end of the fiscal year. They also provided the hospital with an opportunity to do good works.

Carol's less-than-savory boyfriend, someone she called Duane, had tagged along for the delivery. Carol had a death grip on his hand for the first half of her ordeal. Duane told anyone within hearing range that he wasn't the baby's father.

What he was, it became painfully clear just a little while later, as Carol was being taken into recovery, was a junkie. A junkie who was looking to score something. Anything.

With the cleverness that desperation brings, Duane had managed to break into the supply room where the medicines were kept.

Returning from recovery, Sasha was looking for him when she saw Duane trying to sneak out of the room, clutching his jacket to him as if he were smuggling a kitten off the premises.

There were no kittens in the hospital—but there were a lot of valuable things stored in the supply room. Suspicious, Sasha had called out to him. Duane broke into a run immediately. She quickly called for security even as she started running after Duane herself. She'd been the one to bring Carol into the hospital, in her mind that made her responsible for the theft.

Looking at the detective's arm and what was leaking through his clenched fingers, Sasha felt even more responsible for the domino effect her one act of charity had brought about.

"Detective, you're bleeding," she said, horrified.

Tony looked down at his arm. The leather was slashed in two places. "Damn kid ruined my new jacket," he complained heatedly.

Sasha took charge. "Never mind the jacket, he could have ruined you." If there was anger in her voice, it was directed at herself. "Take it off, Detective," she instructed.

He looked at her, mildly amused. "I don't know if we know each other well enough for that, Doc," he deadpanned. The older of the two guards chuckled.

Sasha never even cracked a smile. Her guilt ran deeper than the wound she was looking at. "Hold him for the police," she ordered the security guards who seemed to come to attention at the command. "You—" she looked at the detective "—come with me." She began to lead the way into the E.R.

"You get your medical degree using the G.I. bill?" he asked, following her into the depths of the E.R. When he caught a half-quizzical look from her, he added, "You give orders like a marine."

"Only when I'm met with resistance," she tossed over her shoulder. Waving to a nurse at the nurses' station, she called out, "Eileen, I need a free bed."

Behind her, she heard the detective laugh dryly. "Doc, I'm on duty. Maybe later."

She shot him a silencing look. This wasn't funny. She still didn't know if something vital hadn't been cut, although since he was on his feet, she tended to think not. "Save it," she snapped.

"Number three is empty," Eileen told her, checking the chart located directly behind her on the wall.

"Number three it is." Without missing a step, Sasha headed in that direction. "I'm going to need a suture kit," she added.

"You got it," the nurse replied. By the time Sasha had reached number three, Eileen met them with the requested kit. She paused only long enough to give the doctor's patient an appreciative look, then returned to her post.

"No painkillers," Tony told her tersely. Feeling ill at ease and far from happy about the turn of events,

The Silhouette Reader Service™ — Here's how it works:

Accepting your 2 free books and 2 free gifts places you under no obligation to buy anything. You may keep the books and gifts and return the shipping statement marked "cancel." If you do not cancel, about a month later we'll send you 4 additional books and bill you just $4.24 each in the U.S. or $4.99 each in Canada, plus 25¢ shipping & handling per book and applicable taxes if any.* That's the complete price and — compared to cover prices of $4.99 each in the U.S. and $5.99 each in Canada — it's quite a bargain! You may cancel at any time, but if you choose to continue, every month we'll send you 4 more books, which you may either purchase at the discount price or return to us and cancel your subscription.

*Terms and prices subject to change without notice. Sales tax applicable in N.Y. Canadian residents will be charged applicable provincial taxes and GST. All orders subject to approval. Credit or debit balances in a customer's account(s) may be offset by any other outstanding balance owed by or to the customer. Please allow 4 to 6 weeks for delivery.

If offer card is missing write to: Silhouette Reader Service, 3010 Walden Ave., P.O. Box 1867, Buffalo NY 14240-1867

NO POSTAGE
NECESSARY
IF MAILED
IN THE
UNITED STATES

BUSINESS REPLY MAIL
FIRST-CLASS MAIL   PERMIT NO. 717-003   BUFFALO, NY

POSTAGE WILL BE PAID BY ADDRESSEE

SILHOUETTE READER SERVICE
3010 WALDEN AVE
PO BOX 1867
BUFFALO NY 14240-9952

Do You Have the LUCKY KEY?

PLAY THE Lucky Key Game

and you can get

FREE BOOKS and FREE GIFTS!

Scratch the gold areas with a coin. Then check below to see the books and gifts you can get!

YES!

I have scratched off the gold areas. Please send me the 2 FREE BOOKS and 2 FREE GIFTS for which I qualify. I understand I am under no obligation to purchase any books, as explained on the back of this card.

340 SDL EF6E   240 SDL EF5F

FIRST NAME   LAST NAME

ADDRESS

APT.#   CITY

STATE/ PROV.   ZIP/ POSTAL CODE

www.eHarlequin.com

2 free books plus 2 free gifts   1 free book

2 free books   Try Again!

Offer limited to one per household and not valid to current Silhouette® Romantic Suspense subscribers.
Your Privacy – Silhouette is committed to protecting your privacy. Our Privacy Policy is available online at www.eHarlequin.com or upon request from the Silhouette Reader Service. From time to time we make our lists of customers available to reputable firms who may have a product or service of interest to you. If you would prefer for us not to share your name and address, please check here. ☐

DETACH AND MAIL CARD TODAY!

(S-RS-02/07)

© 2002 HARLEQUIN ENTERPRISES LTD. ® and TM are trademarks owned and used by the trademark owner and/or its licensee.

he perched on the side of the bed, ready to take flight at the slightest provocation.

Sasha lowered the injection she'd prepared. Not giving it was against her better judgment. "It's going to hurt," she warned.

"No painkillers," he repeated. He had to stay focused, alert. Painkillers might take the edge off the pain, but they also took the edge off him. Not a good trade-off. "I don't mind pain. A little bit of pain makes you feel alive."

Threading the needle, she stopped to look at him for a long moment. Reading between the lines and hearing what wasn't being said.

"If that's the only thing that makes you feel alive, Detective, I'd say you have a bigger problem than just a knife wound." Without repeating her instruction, or waiting for him to comply, she placed the needle back on the tray and stepped behind him. He felt her small hands begin to pull his jacket down his shoulders. He shrugged out of the garment, careful not to move his arm any more than he absolutely had to.

He was working with her, Sasha noted with satisfaction. Very gingerly, she slid the jacket down the arm that had been wounded. "It can be fixed," she told him.

That was the whole idea behind his sitting here, preparing to be a pincushion, he thought. "It's just a cut," he pointed out.

Slipping on a fresh set of gloves, she swabbed the

area with antiseptic. Sasha spared him a glance before she took the first stitch. "I meant the jacket. My mother's cousin is a tailor. He can sew and repair anything. You won't even know it was damaged."

She felt him stiffening beneath her hand. "You double as a part-time saleslady?"

"I'm not making a pitch," she informed him. She heard him take in a breath and hold it, even though he was trying to be subtle about it. It was difficult not to grin. Men with their macho pose, she thought.

Tony released the breath he was holding. The pain was manageable if he concentrated on something else. On her. On the way her hair seemed to cascade into her face like a black sea. On the soft, subtle scent that seemed to surround her.

After a beat, his eyes met hers. "I am," he said quietly.

He was what? she wondered. When she couldn't come up with an answer, she decided to ask the question out loud. "Come again?"

"That's part of it," he allowed. Damn, but he was feeling a little light-headed. That shouldn't be happening. It was only a little needle. But the loss of blood, he realized, had not been so little. "Coming here again," he clarified when the confused look on her face only intensified.

"And the pitch?" she prodded, still not certain what he was driving at. He wasn't full of painkillers, but she'd known strong men to pass out at the sight of their own blood.

"Includes coffee," he told her. "And dinner. If you're free." He heard himself talking and was surprised by the sound of his own voice. Maybe he was out of his head, he thought. But he didn't take back the invitation. There was a part of him that wanted to hear what she had to say.

"But I'm not free, Detective." She let the remark sink in, then decided that she'd had enough fun and explained what she really meant. "I'm expensive. At least, that's what my more well-off patients seem to think. And they're right," she confided as she worked another stitch through his flesh. "That way, I can treat and buy medication for my patients who can't afford to pay for any treatment."

She pressed her lips together as she continued stitching up the wound. It went deeper than she'd first thought. Even so, the detective was as immovable as a rock. The only thing that gave him away was the involuntary twitch of his muscles. She was *very* aware of his muscles. It was enough to take her breath away if she wasn't careful, she reproached herself. He needed a doctor right now, not a fan.

She raised her eyes from her work for a split second to look at him. "I'm sorry about this."

Tony made a dismissive noise. "Not exactly your fault."

Now there he was wrong. "But it is. I brought in that thief's girlfriend." The look in his eyes told her he wanted details. So, details he was going to get. It was the least she could do. "I found Carol in the alley right behind the hospital. She was wound up into a ball and grunting. I thought she couldn't make it into PM, you know, labor pains knocking her feet right out from under her, that kind of thing," she explained, all the while working the needle back and forth through his flesh, sewing up first one layer of skin, then the next. "It turned out that she couldn't afford to stay at the hospital, but she wanted to be close by in case the baby was born in some sort of distress." Sasha sighed. "At least she had the presence of mind for that."

"What were you doing in the alley?" he wanted to know.

"Taking a shortcut. My office is in the building right across the street," she reminded him. "The back entrance faces the alley. Anyway, I brought Carol in and this boyfriend—Duane—insisted on coming along. As soon as I had her and the baby wheeled into recovery, he ran off to raid the supply room."

"How'd he get a knife past the security check?" he wanted to know.

Tony forced himself to watch as she worked. The stitches were small, precise, even. Like a seamstress, he thought. Lucky for him. Looks had never meant much to him but if he had a choice between looking like Frankenstein and not, he'd choose not.

"That wasn't a knife. That was a scalpel. He must have lifted it from the delivery room when we weren't looking." She pressed her lips together, aware that he was observing her every move. "Anyway, I owe you."

If anything, she was guilty of having a heart. He didn't see that as a punishable offense. Just an unusual one.

"Okay," he allowed, his voice rumbling along her consciousness, "you pick up the tab for dinner."

"Done," she declared, pulling through the last stitch. She raised her eyes to his. "And done," she repeated, this time more softly, her answer intended as a reply to his suggestion.

Dinner. He was asking her out. Something shimmied through her stomach. It took effort not to place her hand over it. It took further effort not to just turn tail and run from the room, the invitation and the man.

But then, she wouldn't have been Sasha Pulaski, or her father's daughter, so she stayed where she was. And smiled.

Chapter 9

Dinner wound up being postponed.

Not intentionally, but the event was unceremoniously pushed to the rear of Tony's agenda just as he was about to leave the precinct. His plan was to go home, change and then pick the doctor up at her apartment. He had the address tucked into his shirt pocket.

An incoming call changed all that. Directed to Homicide, the call was rerouted to his desk.

"Gonna get that?" he heard Henderson ask as he stared accusingly at the telephone.

"Yeah," Tony bit off, annoyed. He should have left five minutes ago, he told himself. Yanking up the receiver, he pressed it against his ear. "Santini."

He heard the high-pitched voice of the dispatcher say, "There's been another homicide, Detective."

There was *always* another homicide in New York City. That was one of the detractions about living in an overpopulated big city, he thought.

"Have someone else catch it," he'd snapped, his voice overlapping that of the dispatcher's. The woman was rattling off the location where the body had been found. "There're eight other homicide detectives in the squad."

But no apology, no promise of taking her call elsewhere was forthcoming. "Thought you were handling the Hospital Stalker," the woman said.

He hated the name the press had affixed to the killer. It made it seem as if the police had no control over this man.

Well, did they? Tony forced himself to focus on what the dispatcher was saying.

"You just said the body was found in an office across town," he pointed out.

"It was," the woman replied. Then, before he could say anything, she added, "The patrolman who called it in said that the dead man—a doctor—had the same note in his hand."

A doctor. So the killer finally got it right, he thought cynically.

"Give me the address again," Tony instructed. Grabbing the first available piece of paper on his desk, he jotted down the address the woman was reciting. Finished, he terminated the call without bothering with any further exchange. "Henderson," he called over to his partner. "We're up." He heard the man sigh deeply as he lumbered up to his feet. Tony paused and looked at him. "You got somewhere to go?"

Henderson slipped on his hound's-tooth jacket. "Only home." It was obvious that home was where he wanted to be. "Big boxing match on pay-TV tonight."

Tony looked at him incredulously as he waited for the big man to reach him. "You pay to watch two guys beat each other's brains out? Don't you get enough of that here?"

They walked out into the hall together, and then down the corridor to the elevator. "Yeah, but on TV, I don't have to figure out who done it. I already know." He looked at Tony as they got into the elevator. The car had just been standing there, as if it knew it was going to be pressed into service. Henderson made the logical assumption. "Did someone find another body in the hospital?"

Tony shook his head. The elevator made its way down to the first floor without stopping. "No, this time it's across town. And the victim's a doctor."

They weren't called down for every murder. That was why the precinct had as large a squad as it did. "Then how—?"

Tony already knew what Henderson was going to ask. "The patrolman said he found a note."

"Same one?" Henderson asked grimly.

"Same one."

The frown on the man's beefy lips deepened. "Bastard's spreading out."

"Looks like," Tony agreed.

The elevator doors opened and they got out. Darkness wound its fingers around the world outside. And within.

The crime scene had been disturbed, Tony noted.

Despite the best efforts of the inexperienced patrolman who had responded to the initial 911 call, the late doctor's wife had sunk down to the floor, wrapped her arms around the dead man and held him to her. She'd been holding him for the last forty-five minutes.

"What is she doing here?" Tony wanted to know. He put the question to Officer Caldwell. Caldwell looked barely old enough to shave.

"The guy who found him called her. It's a partnership," Officer Caldwell offered. "Seven of them altogether. The Greater Anesthesiologists of New York." The explanation was unnecessary, since that was what it said on the door. "She's his wife," Caldwell added helplessly.

The woman was sobbing now as she rocked to and fro. Her arms were locked in a death grip around her husband. There was blood smeared on her coat, her black slacks and her sweater.

The crime scene investigators were going to have a fit, Tony thought. Making his way over to her, he politely addressed the woman.

"Ma'am, I need you to get up." She gave no indication that she heard him or was even aware of his presence. Tony tried again. "Ma'am?"

Trapped in a world whose walls were comprised of grief, the slain physician's wife didn't seem to hear him. For the time being, since the damage was already done, Tony backed away, allowing her to hold onto her husband for a while longer.

He looked over toward a very distraught man in his mid to late thirties. The man's haircut and suit alone would have set him back three months' salary, Tony mused as he crossed to him.

"You were the one who found him?" Tony asked.

The physician nodded. "Dr. Tyler Harris," he said numbly.

The name seemed to be free-floating in space. "Is that your name or his?"

The doctor blinked, as if that helped him process the question. It took a moment for him to respond. "His. Mine's Rothenberg. Julian," he added as an afterthought, then said his whole name. "Dr. Julian Rothenberg. I just looked in to say good night to Ty as I was leaving and there he was." He gestured haplessly toward the body. "Like that."

Someone had to have seen or heard something, Tony thought. "Did you see anyone leave the office?"

But Rothenberg shook his head. "I was busy in the back." He paused, then said, "Maybe Myra noticed someone…"

"Myra?" Henderson asked. Until now, Tony's partner had merely stood in his shadow, listening. Looking around. Tony knew the older detective was processing the scene in his own way.

"Our receptionist," Rothenberg clarified. "Oh, wait, Myra took off after lunch."

Tony exchanged looks with Henderson. "In the middle of the day?" That seemed a little unusual to him. Was it just a coincidence, or had Myra possibly been notified that something was going down? "Anyone covering for her?"

The doctor shook his head. "Myra does the billing, mostly and keeps tabs on the surgeries being scheduled. We're not those kind of doctors."

It sounded like an odd thing to say. "What kind?" Henderson wanted to know.

"The kind who see patients in our office. We see them in the hospital, the day of the surgery. And we usually call the night before to go over things with them," he added, then explained, "but no one ever comes to the office."

Tony looked around. He was no expert, but he knew expensive when he saw it. "Pretty elaborate decorating for a place no one ever sees."

"We see it," Dr. Rothenberg pointed out. There was just enough snobbery in his voice to be off-putting.

"Yeah, right," Tony muttered under his breath. He took out his notepad and flipped to an empty page. "What hospital was Dr. Harris with?"

"The group is affiliated with several hospitals,"

Rothenberg told him. When Tony continued to look at him expectantly, the doctor rattled off the names of the hospitals.

None of them were Patience Memorial.

Where was the connection? Tony wondered. *Was* there a connection or just some psycho running around, terrorizing people? "Did Harris ever freelance? Fill in for another anesthesiologist?" Tony asked.

Rothenberg didn't look as if he was sure what he was being asked. "We cover for each other if some kind of emergency arises, but those are the only hospitals we're affiliated with. Why?" And then genuine fear contoured his features. "Does this have anything to do with the Hospital Stalker?"

Tony didn't answer him directly. Instead, he said, "The other three victims were associated with Patience Memorial Hospital."

Rothenberg's head bobbed up and down, as if everything was making perfect sense to him. "Tyler's last group was associated with that hospital."

"Last group?" Tony repeated.

On firmer ground, Rothenberg looked a shade more confident again. "Doctors recruit just like everyone else, Detective. As an anesthesiologist, Tyler had an excellent record. Better than most. We made him an offer he couldn't refuse."

"Looks like the killer did, too," Tony commented more to Henderson than to Rothenberg as he looked down at the dead man.

* * *

Sasha tossed the magazine she'd restlessly been paging through for the last twenty minutes onto the coffee table. If pressed, she wouldn't have been able to repeat a single thing she'd read.

Pretty bad for a woman with a photographic memory, she thought ruefully.

She resisted looking at the clock again. It had to be approaching ten o'clock, or perhaps even later. That would make Santini three hours late. If he were coming, which, it seemed, he wasn't.

The detective had told her that he would be at her apartment by seven. He hadn't come, hadn't called. Obviously, she'd slipped his mind. Or maybe he'd thought better of his invitation.

Sasha frowned, telling herself not to make a big deal out of it. But she'd never been stood up before, she thought.

It didn't matter, she silently insisted, except that she had been looking forward to going out to some place different for a change. These days, "going out" meant going back home to Queens, to the house where she'd grown up, to spend time with her parents and younger sisters. That is, if Tatania and Marja were home. These days, that usually wasn't the case. Tatania was an intern. Asserting her independence, she'd chosen a hospital that *wasn't* Patience Memorial and right now, Sasha was secretly glad that Tatania was somewhere else. As for Marja, the youngest of the Pulaski sisters, she was in her last year of medical school. Free time for either of them was rare.

The apartment was too quiet, Sasha thought. So quiet she could swear she could hear the paint aging on the walls. Ordinarily, one or both of her other sisters were here, barring some last-minute emergency at the hospital. But Natalya had gone off with a couple of friends to spend a hard-earned weekend in Atlantic City and Kady, well God only knew what Kady was doing. The most rebellious sister of the group, Kady liked to come and go as she pleased "without having to punch a clock," as she put it. The remark was a blatant reference to all those times as teenagers when they'd had to account for themselves to their father.

It wasn't so much that Josef Pulaski was unreasonably strict, he just worried about them. As a policeman, he'd been privy to the lowest forms of humanity and more than anything, he wanted to keep his wife and daughters safe from that world.

It was a sweet sentiment, she thought. Confining, but nonetheless a sweet sentiment.

Sasha blew out a breath, looking around for the umpteenth time. Here she was, with the apartment all to herself and nothing to do.

She supposed it was better this way. If the detective had taken her out, he might have insisted on walking her back home. Since it was empty, she might have been tempted to ask him in....

Tempted, now there was a word she hadn't used

in a long time, Sasha thought. That was because she hadn't felt that way in a long time.

Tempted.

She hadn't been tempted by anyone or anything since Adam had been killed. Hadn't felt anything since he'd been killed. Nothing except for a sense of duty.

Until now.

Not now, she insisted silently.

Rotating her neck from side to side, she rose from the sofa. As she did, she slanted a glance at the clock above the TV monitor. It *was* past ten. Maybe what she should do was go to bed before one of those babies she was scheduled to bring into the world in the next few weeks decided to pop early. God knew she was always complaining about never getting enough sleep. Now was her chance to catch up.

It was as good a plan as any.

Sasha switched off the light in the living room and reduced the lamp closest to the hallway down to its lowest setting. That way, the small foyer would have some illumination in case Kady came home before dawn.

She was on her way to her bedroom when she heard the doorbell ring.

Instantly, every muscle in her body tightened. Thoughts of those two murdered nurses, not to mention poor Jorge, were never all that far from her thoughts. She stared at the front door.

The killer hasn't changed his MO, Sash. He's not

going from door to door ringing doorbells like some demonic trick-or-treater, she upbraided herself.

Nonetheless, she made no effort to cross to the foyer.

When the doorbell rang again, Sasha was forced to abandon the idea that if she simply ignored the person, whoever was ringing her doorbell would just go away.

It was probably just one of her sisters' boyfriends, looking for them, Sasha reasoned. Squaring her shoulders, she approached the door.

"Who is it?"

There was a pause, as if the person on the other side of the door didn't know what to call himself.

The murderer?

A chill raced down her spine. Deciding that it was better to be safe than sorry, Sasha pulled out the cell phone she kept in her pocket at all times and quickly pressed the buttons that would connect her to Santini. The detective had picked a hell of a time to stand her up, she thought, annoyed.

The second she pressed Send, Sasha heard a phone ringing somewhere in the hallway outside her apartment. With the cell phone still against her ear, she looked through the peephole. And saw the man she was calling standing on the other side of her door.

"Detective?"

With one hand braced against the side of the peephole, Tony leaned against the door. "Look, I know it's late, but could you open up the door, Sasha?"

Sasha. She suddenly realized that in all the exchanges they'd had, Santini had never called her by her given name before. It kind of rumbled from his mouth, she thought, amused despite the fact that she knew she was supposed to be really annoyed.

She slipped her cell phone back in her pocket. Flipping open the lock, she removed the chain and then opened the door.

"Someone steal your watch, Detective?" she asked politely as she stepped back.

Tony walked in, feeling awkward. Knowing he'd only feel more awkward if he'd skipped coming here and gone directly home from the crime scene.

He held up his left hand, allowing her to glimpse the watch that was strapped to his wrist. The watch that he only removed when he showered.

"No, it's still there." He dropped his hand to his side again as he turned to look at her. "I forgot about picking you up for dinner."

Sasha closed the door. "Now there's something every woman loves to hear," she commented drolly. "That she's forgettable."

Sasha Pulaski might be many things, Tony thought, trying not to stare at the way the electric-blue dress she had on clung to the outline of her breasts, but forgettable was certainly not one of them.

He tried again. "The reason I forgot," he told her, "was because there's been another homicide."

Every other thought flew from her mind, crowded

out by horror as she looked at him. "At the hospital? When? Who?"

She was firing questions at him like a seasoned veteran at a target range. Taking a deep breathe he addressed the first one. "No, not at the hospital. At the Greater Anesthesiologists of New York's office."

That wasn't good, she thought. She felt a chill had gripped her heart. She already had patients who wanted to know if they could deliver their baby at another hospital. People were getting leery of PM. "The killer's spreading out his base?"

In response, Tony shook his head. "I don't think so."

"But you just said—"

"The victim was a doctor," he told her. "Dr. Tyler Harris."

Sasha's eyes widened in disbelief. This was becoming very, very weird. "Ty?"

"You knew him?" It was a rhetorical question, given the tone of her voice.

"Everyone knew him." She couldn't believe it. Ty, who liked being the center of every gathering. Ty, who was funny and gregarious. *Murdered.* It just didn't seem possible. "He was one of those people who had a story for everything and was willing to share it at the drop of a hat." A bittersweet smile twisted her lips. "They used to say that he didn't need to bother with applying anesthesia, he could just talk the patient to sleep." The nightmare was escalating. "When did it happen?"

"One of his associates found the body at five." Tony looked around. Her apartment looked warm, homey, with just enough scattered around to give it a lived-in look. In contrast, his apartment was as personal as a bus depot. "He called the police and then the doctor's wife. We found Mrs. Harris holding him when we arrived."

Maybe it wasn't the same person who had killed the people at PM. "He was still alive?"

Santini's expression was grim as he said, "No."

His meaning sank in. She looked at him in horror. "Oh God, that poor woman."

Interest entered his eyes. "You were acquainted with her?"

She didn't want him to misunderstand. "Only by reputation. Hers," she emphasized. "Linda Harris is a very jealous, suspicious woman. She thought that every woman in the room was after her husband, that every woman was out to take him away from her." Sasha's words played back to her in her head. "I guess now she won't have to worry about that."

"Jealousy." Santini said the word as if he was chewing on it. Sasha looked at him. "Ordinarily, that would be a motive for us to explore."

Tyler Harris's wife was a shrew, but she didn't think that the woman was capable of murder. Still, she wondered about Santini's reasoning. "But?"

"But," and it was an all-important *but,* "Harris had one of those notes in his hand. Or on the floor next to him, actually." That was where the note had been when he'd arrived on the scene. "The patrolman who was there first said that Mrs. Harris pulled the paper out of the doctor's hand, thinking it was some kind of suicide note."

Or love note, Sasha thought. That was probably what was running through the woman's mind. "Any chance that she planted the note?"

He couldn't help the weary smile that came to his lips. She was making noises like a police detective. "The note's not a piece of common knowledge. We've kept that from the media."

She knew how that worked. The police held back some small, telling piece of information that only the killer would know. "Smart."

"Thanks." He was enjoying this bit of conversation and reminded himself that he'd come here to apologize for not showing up at seven, and then he'd go home. He'd done the former, in a fashion. But for some reason, he couldn't quite get himself to follow through on the latter. He didn't want to go home to his studio apartment, to the emptiness. Not yet. "Any chance I might be able to get a cup of coffee?"

According to the rules of engagement set down by Rita Riley, her best friend in college, Sasha knew that she was supposed to be indignant at how easily she'd slipped his mind. In keeping with that, she should be showing him the door. But then again, last time she'd heard, Rita was on her way to divorce court for a second time.

Sasha smiled and nodded. "I think the odds are pretty favorable. Come with me."

Turning on her heel, she led the way to the kitchen. The woman, Tony noted almost against his will as he followed her, looked almost as good going as she did coming.

Chapter 10

Tony sat down on the outermost stool and rested his hands on the counter. It wasn't a kitchen that had room for a table, but it was a bright, cheery-looking space, even under artificial light. It seemed hard to imagine that creatures like serial killers and stalkers existed in the same world occupied by someone like Sasha Pulaski.

For a moment, there was no other sound than that of the coffeemaker, percolating. He watched Sasha stretch as she reached up into the cupboard for two mugs. There didn't appear to be an ounce of excess fat on her. He wondered when she found time to work out, given her schedule.

Rousing himself, Tony focused on the reason he'd

been late. The anesthesiologist no longer worked at Patience Memorial, yet he'd been killed. It seemed to him that everyone associated with the hospital was at risk.

"You know," Tony finally began, measuring out his words slowly, "maybe you should go on vacation for a while."

The mugs secured, she turned around and placed both on the counter beside the coffee machine. Amusement curved her lips. "Are you proposition-ing me, Detective, or trying to get rid of me?"

If her question surprised him, he didn't show it. "Neither. I'm just trying to keep you safe."

She looked at him for a long moment. A warm feeling descended over her, wrapping her in its arms before dissolving again. She smiled at him.

"Thanks for the thought, but that's just what we're trying to avoid at PM—a mass exodus by the staff." The last few weeks, especially after finding the orderly, had been hell. This newest development was just going to make things worse. But she had no desire to flee. Only a fierce desire to catch whoever was responsible for the killings. "It's bad enough that the patients are getting jittery."

Other than looking into whether any patients had lodged complaints against any of the victims, he hadn't given the patients at the hospital much thought.

"Oh?"

Sasha nodded. Because the coffee was still brew-ing, she leaned forward over the counter, sharing a moment with him. "I've had some of mine ask if they could deliver their babies at another hospital."

"This guy's not killing patients," he pointed out, "just staff members."

"Still not a warm and toasty thing to contemplate." Sasha searched his face for any additional clues. "You think it's a man?"

He tended to think of all brutal crimes in terms of men having committed them. He supposed, in a way, there was a bit of the old-fashioned chauvinist left within him. The department shrink would have accused him of being sexist. "Most serial killers are."

Sasha recalled one of the books her father had in his library. It was an encyclopedia of serial killers. All aspects of law enforcement had always fascinated her father. "But not all."

"No," he allowed, "not all."

The coffee machine had settled down. Sasha took the pot and filled first his mug and then her own. With an economy of movement, she set out a container of milk and placed the sugar bowl within his reach. Santini ignored both. He liked his coffee like his world—black.

She added enough milk into her coffee to make it turn into a light shade of chocolate. She took a sip before asking, "Have you eaten?" And then she flashed a smile that was just a tinge rueful. For a second, in light of the newest development, she'd almost forgotten. "No, of course you haven't." And he had the look of a hungry man about him, she thought. "I can throw something together for you."

Tony shook his head, taking another long sip of the black liquid and letting it course through his veins. "You don't have to bother." It wasn't meant so much as a protest as a dismissal. "Coffee's fine."

Her parents had always emphasized the importance of hospitality to her. Even when they had next to nothing, they always made it a point to share with anyone who came to their door. Her smile broadened. "No bother," she assured him.

Another, more forceful protest rose to his lips, but died there for lack of conviction; he was hungry and the only thing in his refrigerator was a third of a loaf of bread. The last time he'd looked, the slices were tinged with green and growing greener.

Closing the refrigerator with her elbow, Sasha deposited two kinds of peppers, green and red, and a package of chicken onto the counter. She turned her attention to the crowded carousel of spices in the corner and began selecting containers.

"How do you feel about curried chicken?" she asked him, her voice echoing from inside the lower cabinet as she squatted there, locating the largest frying pan she had.

Her bounty in her hand, Sasha rose again and placed the pan on the largest burner when he didn't answer. She slanted a glance in his direction.

"Never thought about it one way or another," he told her with a shrug.

She put her own interpretation to his words. Taking a drop of oil, she jiggled the pan until the single drop coated the surface.

"Never had it?" was her conclusion.

She was good, he thought, then shook his head. "Not that I recall."

Like a child facing the prospect of a new toy, she grinned. "Ah, a fresh palate. This should be fun." Recruiting a heavy chopping block, she began dicing peppers with a steady rhythm he found almost hypnotic. She made quick work of the peppers and turned her attention to the chicken. "So, Detective," she began cheerfully. "What's your story?"

He thought they'd already covered that. But since she had given him coffee and was determined to feed him, he decided to humor her to an extent. "I just told you. There was another homicide and—"

Sasha looked up at him. The rest of the sentence disappeared. He lost his train of thought as he felt something stir inside him again. Damn it, he was overtired, he thought. Overtired and stimulated at the same time. Not a good combination, he told himself. Cops got sloppy when they were both. And he couldn't afford to get sloppy. On or off the job.

"No," Sasha countered firmly, shaking her head at what he was about to say. "*Your* story," she emphasized. When he said nothing, she tried again. "What's behind the badge, Santini?"

His eyes met hers when she turned to look at him. "Muscle and bone."

It was, she thought, like playing chess. He blocked her every move. "You ask a lot of questions, but you never answer any."

"Maybe because the answers don't make a difference." He didn't welcome people into his life. There were no invitations issued. Not anymore.

Meaning his answers would be evasive. She didn't want him to evade her. She wanted the truth.

"The answers always make a difference," she told him, then paused as she studied his face. "Who are you, Detective Santini?"

"Just a guy trying to get to the bottom of things."

He was defining himself by his work. But there was more to him than that. Much more.

"When you're not trying to get to the bottom of things," she insisted. "What makes you laugh?"

That was simple enough to answer. "I don't laugh." The last time he had, it was with Annie, over some silly thing she'd done.

Sasha stopped chopping. Her hand on her hip, she looked at him for a long moment. When she spoke, her voice was filled with compassion. And understanding. Because she'd been there herself. "You need to change that, Detective Santini."

Watching Sasha move around the tiny kitchen brought back memories. Memories that he'd thought he'd buried when Annie had been taken from him. But being here with this woman tonight after a long, hard day, sipping coffee and watching her prepare a meal, felt damn near normal.

When was the last time he'd felt normal? When had he felt like something other than a machine, going through the paces because he knew if he stopped he couldn't go on? Couldn't go on because he'd been to the other side, been allowed to glimpse what life could be like for him, and now he missed it like hell.

But that was for only him to know. Him and no one else. Not even a woman with hair the color of midnight and a smile that cut clear down to the bone.

"Maybe," he said very slowly, toying with what was left in his cup, "for the space of the evening you could stop calling me Detective Santini."

"Fine." Pausing, she poured him a fresh cup, then continued working. "What would you like me to call you?"

"My given name's Anthony," he reminded her.

"Anthony," she repeated with a nod, saying the name as if she was tasting it, one letter at a time. "Yes, I remember. Tony." A smile seemed to vibrate around the name. "I'm Sasha."

A small ring formed beneath the mug. Tony erased it with his thumb, then set the mug back on the counter. "I know."

She hadn't meant to suggest that he'd forgotten it. Sasha had no doubt that somewhere within the recesses of his memory, Detective Santini could access everything he'd ever come across.

"I meant, for tonight. You keep calling me Doctor." They were both guilty of trying to keep their distance. She no longer wanted to. "Maybe we should both stop standing behind our titles."

The moment seemed to stretch out forever. "Maybe," he allowed.

He was agreeing, but Sasha heard the caution in his voice. Swiftly, she gathered up everything on the chopping block and deposited it into the frying pan. Turning the heat up, she stirred the peppers, chicken and onions together, then began adding the battalion of spices, one by one.

A smile feathered along the corners of her mouth. She slanted another look at him as she stirred. "Now tell me something personal."

Maybe coming here was a bad idea after all. Something had drawn him here. The need to apologize for not calling wasn't the real reason. He could have left a message on her answering machine if that were the case.

He'd wanted to see her. And now, he was paying the price. "What?"

She lowered the heat and covered the pan. "Well, for all intents, this is a date." Saying the word felt strange. And yet, what else could she honestly call this? "We've known each other for what, six weeks now?" She didn't wait for affirmation. She knew exactly how long she'd known Tony. "I think it's time we shared something more than coffee." Lifting the lid, she stirred once, then replaced it again. "So, tell me something personal."

The coffee cup was empty. He debated taking a

third mugful, then decided against it. "You're a very attractive woman."

He wasn't going to get away that easily. "Something personal about you."

"I'm *not* a very attractive woman," he responded gamely.

Sasha laughed and shook her head. He was a challenge, she'd give him that.

"Okay, I'll go first." And then she sobered just a little, the way she always did when she thought about Adam and how quickly his life had been cut short. "My fiancé's name was Adam and I thought I was going to die when he did. I almost did, inside."

"What brought you around?"

"My parents and sisters." If it hadn't been for them, that dark place she'd slipped into would never have let her go. "Adam was my first and only real relationship. That night in the hospital parking structure, when I first saw Angela, it brought it all back to me." She took a deep breath, realizing she'd gotten far too serious. "You have to find who's doing this."

There was no doubt in his mind how this would be resolved. "We will."

The smile she flashed told him that she believed him. He would have thought an intelligent woman would have been more skeptical.

"Okay," she said, stirring again. "Your turn."

He didn't want a turn. Didn't want to bare his soul to anyone. He'd long since left behind the notion that confession was good for the soul—if he'd ever believed it in the first place.

"I didn't agree to this game."

She heard things in his voice, heard barriers being reinforced. Her heart went out to him.

"What are you afraid of, Tony?" she asked softly.

"Same thing you are."

She turned down the heat beneath the frying pan even further, allowing the ingredients to simmer, before she turned all her attention to him.

"You're afraid of feeling something again?" Before he could shut out her questions, she came around the counter to stand next to him. "That's the only way we have of proving that we're alive, Tony. Feeling."

Feelings were highly overrated, he thought. "I'll prove I'm alive by catching this bastard."

"And then the next one? And the next one after that?" she guessed.

Now she understood, he thought. "Yes."

He was running. Hiding from himself. Just as she had been, she thought. Even now, there was this urge to flee. But she knew she couldn't give in to it. She had to stand up in order not to be dragged down. "When do you have time for you?"

Maybe he'd given her too much credit. He would have thought she would have caught on by now. "With any luck, I won't."

Sasha didn't back away. Her eyes looked into his. Seeing herself there. "You can't outrun it."

"It?" he mocked, his manner meant to get her to back away.

He knew perfectly well what she was talking about, she thought. "The pain. You have to come to terms with it and move on."

He hated people who thought they knew what was best for you. Even beautiful people. "Have you?" he challenged, turning the tables on her.

She surprised him by saying, "To some extent. Doesn't mean I love Adam any the less," she added quickly, "just that I didn't shut down my heart. All systems are still up and running."

"Good for you." The response was meant to be dismissive.

"Yes," Sasha said quietly, "it is."

She was still standing near him, so close that their breath was mingling, that her words could have fit into his. He needed only to reach up, to cup the back of her head and bring his mouth down to hers. The debate raged hot and heavy for a few moments. He managed to refrain, but it wasn't easy.

She could almost read his mind. Or was that wishful thinking on her part? Anticipation laced fingers with a jittery panic. Finally, Sasha stepped back. "Dinner's ready."

He wanted to say the hell with dinner. He wanted to act on this feeling that was suddenly surging through him before he could think better of it. Before he could stop himself again. There was a tiny part of him that ached to feel again. To recapture what he'd once had.

But that was impossible and he knew it. He wasn't one of those men who fell easily into love. He was one of those men who had to be ambushed by it, to be captured and taken prisoner. It had happened once. He damn well doubted that it would ever happen again.

"This is good."

The compliment was almost grudgingly given, following several minutes of silence while they both sat at the counter.

"Thanks." She wanted to ask why he looked so surprised, but she decided to hold off. Maybe he'd actually offer a little more conversation on his own.

And he did after another two minutes had passed. "Where you'd learn to cook like this?"

"It's in the genes," she told him with a grin. "My mother can almost literally create something out of nothing. When I was growing up, there was no money for things like prepackaged meals and frozen entrées. Mama would come up with meals using whatever she could find at home in the pantry." A fond look came into her eyes. "Mama was right up there with the miracle of the fishes and loaves. I think, if I hadn't gone into medicine, I might have opted to start my own restaurant."

He had her pegged right. She was a dreamer. "Most businesses fail in their first year," he told her, his attention devoted to his meal. He hadn't realized he was this hungry until he'd begun to eat. "Those that don't usually fold in the first five."

Sasha blew out a long breath. "You have got to be the least cheerful person I have ever met," she commented. And that bothered her. "Don't you ever see the upside of anything?"

"I did, once," he admitted in what he felt, in the next second, was a moment of weakness.

He didn't make it a habit of admitting things to people, of letting them into his head. Not even his brothers. But there was something about this woman, something that warmed him. That tempted him. That stood at the door of his self-imposed prison and threatened to splinter the wood.

"So what happened?" she asked, her voice low, coaxing. Understanding.

He knew she was asking about his wife. About the circumstances that took her from him. This was where he slid off the stool, said something like thanks and went on his way.

Except he didn't.

"She died," he heard himself saying. "In a hit-and-run accident. Whoever hit her just left her there, on the side of the road. When she died," he said heavily, feeling the ache all over again, "everything else did too."

Sasha placed her hand over his, one grieving soul touching another.

"I'm so sorry," she whispered.

When he raised his eyes to hers, he knew that she was serious. That she wasn't just mouthing empty words. And that spoke to him.

Her eyes still on his, Sasha brushed her fingers along his cheek. He felt as if something broke loose inside. Rising, he drew her up to her feet with him. The next moment, he took her face in his hands and kissed her. Kissed her because something inside of him hurt so badly, he could hardly stand it. Kissed her because he wanted to put an end to that ache.

As he brushed his lips against hers, something rose up from the depths of him and seemed to explode. The sweetness he discovered on her lips caused him to deepen the kiss. To fall headlong into it.

And with each passing fraction of a second, the power increased. The pull drew him into the very center of this unexpected hurricane that had suddenly risen up all around him.

She felt soft against him.

Her body seemed to fit right into his, so much so that it was as if they had been created as two complementary puzzle pieces.

What the hell was he doing? Another second and he'd drop off the face of the earth, go plummeting over the side of the abyss that he hadn't even suspected was there. Kissing her wasn't just a pleasurable experience, it was an experience that defied description, defied being pigeonholed. And he wanted to take it to the next plateau.

With a burst of superhuman energy, Tony forced himself to pull back. He felt shaken. The air that he sucked into his lungs didn't steady anything.

"I'm sorry. I had no right to do that. I'll go. Thanks for the meal."

She felt as if the short sentences were attacking her, one after another, as Tony drew back making his way toward the door. Away from her.

Snapping to, Sasha quickly caught up to him before he could leave.

She began at the end and worked her way to the beginning. "You're welcome for the meal. You don't have to leave. And you have every right to do that. There's no reason to be sorry." She looked at him pointedly. "I wanted you to kiss me."

"Look—" He felt as if he was stumbling over a tongue that had somehow gotten to be five feet long and incredibly unwieldy. "—you're vulnerable—"

There was no denying that, Sasha thought. Today marked five years since she'd gotten engaged to Adam and maybe, in between all the patients she had seen today during her hectic schedule, she'd been feeling sorry for herself.

But she'd meant what she'd said. It was time to move forward. At least a little. Denying herself the right to feel was cruel and unusual punishment. It was time to stop beating herself up because she was still alive and Adam was not.

Adam wouldn't have wanted that.

"Yes, I am," she agreed, wrapping her arms

around Tony's neck and once again drawing herself
closer to him than a soft whisper. "But don't worry,"
she added, rising up on her toes, bringing her lips
close to his. "It's not catching."

He didn't know about that, he thought, taking
what was offered.

But, catching or not, he had no choice but to do
what every fiber in his body begged him to do.

He brought his mouth down on hers and utterly
shattered every promise he'd made to himself about
keeping his distance and remaining uninvolved.

Chapter 11

Sasha made him feel strong and weak at the same time. Powerful, invincible and yet completely vulnerable and exposed. Had he been able to think, Tony would have said that the woman in his arms had turned him inside out and spun him around until he wasn't sure which end was up.

But thinking was the last thing he was capable of right now. Not with this myriad of sensations bombarding him from every conceivable direction. And at the very center of the emotional hurricane that was raging within him was desire. Desire, fiery and strong and so unrelenting that he couldn't even manage to draw a complete breath without every fiber of his being shouting that he wanted her.

Where had all this come from?

Had it been hiding in the wings, waiting to capture him while he was still unaware?

But that was just it, he *was* aware, aware of every nuance of her body, every movement, every curve that called to him. He hadn't felt this vibrant, this alive since Annie had been in his life.

He felt like exploding.

It took everything he had within him not to give in to what was happening, not to quickly take this woman who stirred him so much. The hunger that seemed to have risen out of the shadows and taken him prisoner begged to be satiated.

With extraordinary effort, he banked it down as best he could. He wasn't some rutting pig, some soulless, lusting beast who suddenly had an appetite that needed satisfying. He was a man, a man who could think, who could reason. Who could exercise control over himself.

The last thing he wanted was to frighten Sasha. Or offend her.

So he caressed her, kissed her and gave up part of his resistance. He found himself lost in the taste of her. In the feel, the scent, the softness of her. From where he stood, it was a good bargain.

Tony hardly remembered how they managed to get from the stool to the sofa. All he knew was that the second he'd begun kissing her, he couldn't pull himself away, couldn't stand back and create that small, necessary distance he'd always been able to maintain. There'd always been a part of him that could observe, that could separate him from what was going on. Even with Annie, he was able to maintain that small, uninvaded space.

That space didn't exist any more. He couldn't find it, couldn't take refuge in it. He was hopelessly lost in her.

Tony kissed her mouth, her face, her throat and all the while his hands roamed over her body, memorizing every subtle curve, every inviting dip, every single hollow that he found.

And even while he was losing himself in her, Tony could feel her fingers as they worked the buttons from their holes on his shirt, heard her deep intake of breath as she dragged the shirt from his waist, then pushed it from his torso. Felt his own breath catch in his throat as her fingertips moved along his chest, his skin. Branding him.

This was wrong.

He shouldn't be letting this happen, his mind argued silently. Shouldn't be with her like this. And yet, he wanted nothing more. Even though it shattered every single promise, broke every rule, tore him out of his solitary cell where he'd been bathed in darkness.

She made him feel alive. Feel glad to *be* alive. He didn't even have time to feel disloyal to Annie.

Everything seemed to be happening in some sort of warm haze. And yet, he was aware of everything. Aware of the feel of her lips, the silkiness of her skin, the zipper as it flowed down her back. Aware of her dress as it floated away from her body and to the floor.

He was supposed to stop now. It had gotten out of hand.

He hadn't meant for this to happen when he'd taken that right turn down the street that led to her apartment building. He'd only meant to offer his apologies for neglecting to call her earlier and then go. That was all. Nothing more.

Liar.

The word vibrated in his brain, mocking him. And then it disappeared, burned away in the heat of his desire.

She was naked and beautiful and, for this single, precious moment in time, his. And he wanted her with a need that was almost uncontrollable.

A small kernel of feeling that was deeply rooted within him demanded that he hold off taking her, hold off from the ultimate moment. It demanded that he do his very best to place her needs before his own. It wasn't a conscious thought, more like a sense of order. Of how things had to be, to be right.

It wasn't until Tony's lips touched hers that she realized just how much she had ached for this. How much she'd truly missed the physical aspects of a good relationship. Since Adam had died, there had been no one to take his place, no one to turn to. To escape the grief, the pain, she had buried herself in her work. Pretending that it and her family were enough. That she had no other needs, no great desire to savor the physical pleasures that came from loving and being loved by a man.

There'd been men since Adam had died, men who had been interested in her. But she'd refused any attempts on their part to get closer. She'd become celibate because making love had always been just that to her, making love. Not having sex. Adam had been her first, her only. It was because she'd loved him that she'd made love with him. It had been a natural outpouring. Her love had just spilled out, impossible to contain or manage any longer without an outlet.

That couldn't be the case here, she thought, even as her body heated in response to Tony's touch. She didn't love this detective. She felt for him. Related to him and was drawn to him because of the similar circumstances in their backgrounds. And because of the life-and-death situation they found themselves on the edge of. Tony was a protector and she appreciated that, but it wasn't as if she actually needed protecting.

What she needed, she realized, was to feel like a woman again. A desirable woman. And if she were being honest with herself, he made her feel just that. From the first covert look of interest in his eyes when he'd slanted a glance in her direction, something electric had telegraphed itself to her, slicing through protocol, through logic. Through all the barriers she'd constructed around herself. She'd wanted Tony long before she'd given in to him.

His tenderness surprised her. Touched her. More than she could ever say. She'd thought to get lost in the wild rapture that would overtake her the moment they came together, but he somehow managed to be tender within the frenzy that seized them, the frenzy that sent clothes flying, along with any lingering inhibitions she might have possessed.

But it wasn't a wild flash in the pan, a simple wham-bam-thank-you-ma'am. It was so much more.

The taste of his lips inflamed her. His breath sent her pulse racing even faster than it already was, stirring every dormant thing inside her. There was an overwhelming need to be swept away and another, equally great need not to drown within the tidal wave that had been created.

She needed to make Tony feel something as well, needed to leave a mark, an impression on his soul that would make her different in his eyes, different from all the other women she assumed he had had over the years.

Grasping his arms, she caught him off guard and reversed their positions before he realized what she was doing. She scrambled up, moving until she was on top of him. The flicker of surprise in his gray eyes pleased her to no end.

Sasha lost no time. She dusted his chest with kisses, snaking her body along his. Succeeding, she thought triumphantly, in arousing him to an even greater level. She knew she was on borrowed time, that any second, he would be taking over again. He was already making her head spin and there was a rushing noise in her ears that continued to grow louder. There was no doubt that at any moment, she was going to lose control and she wanted desperately to bring him up to as high a plateau as she could before that happened.

And, just as she had come to both her own limit and his, Tony suddenly reversed their positions again. And then he was the one looming over her. He laced his hands with hers, holding them overhead and then to the side as he worked his mouth slowly down her torso.

Electrical charges shot through her. Sasha twisted and wiggled both into the sensations and away from them. Trying to savor, to sustain. Trying to forestall the ultimate detonation, keeping it back for just a little longer.

He was smiling, as he raised himself back over her again. Her whole body was humming like a newly tuned generator, but it was his smile that registered most of all. His smile that had the greatest effect on her.

And then he was inside her and they were one. One and racing together to the final destination. The final summit before they plunged back down to the earth that was waiting for them.

The sound of Sasha's growing agitation, released in small gasps and garbled words that completely defied understanding, excited Tony to a point he was completely unfamiliar with.

And then the explosion came, wrapping itself around them both. Sealing them together in desire and sweat. They hung suspended in midair.

Sasha felt part of Tony's weight against her. Felt her heart hammering so hard, she was certain it would pop out of her chest and into his. She wrapped her legs around his, unwilling to have the moment end, even after it had.

The descent was slow, but inevitable. When she felt him roll off, the emptiness hovered on the brink of her consciousness, threatening to oppress her. She held it at bay as best she could.

What felt like a hundred years later, Tony propped himself up on his elbow and leaned his head against his hand. She could feel him looking at her for a long moment. When she finally turned her head toward him, she couldn't read his expression. Was he angry? Pleased? As blown away as she was?

"Why?" he asked.

"Why what?" Sasha managed to push the words out after one failed attempt. Her throat was so dry, it felt as if it was sticking to itself, sealing off almost all of her air.

He didn't explain, didn't enlighten. All he did was repeat the question. "Why?"

She didn't know why. All she knew was that if she hadn't, she would have burst into flames on her own. Until it had happened, she hadn't known how much she had wanted it to happen. But that was all too serious, too much to burden him with. There were no strings here.

So she forced a smile to her lips and said, "I didn't have any dessert to offer you."

Her flippant response surprised him. He didn't think she was capable of flippant answers. But then, he wouldn't have thought her capable of what had just happened here, either.

No, that wasn't exactly right. He'd felt, sensed really, that beneath her cool exterior there was a passionate, vibrant woman. What he hadn't been prepared for was the degree to which that was true. And was unequally unprepared for his own reaction to her. Granted he'd been attracted to her, maybe even from the very start, but the degree to which he'd found himself responding had caught him completely off guard.

Even now, spent and exhausted, Tony could feel the beginnings of desire starting to stir him. Could feel himself wanting her all over again. It didn't seem possible and yet, there it was. Desire, fully clothed and waiting to be stripped down to its barest essence all over again.

"That's one hell of a menu," he finally said in response to her comment.

She smiled. She felt very close to him at this moment and the fact that they were both naked, their flesh warm from the press of feverish skin against skin, had nothing to do with it. It was the honesty and not the proximity that made her feel so close to him.

"Yes, it kind of surprised me, too." Moving on instincts, Sasha turned her body into his.

Tony felt himself responding even more fiercely to her than before. It was no longer simply mind over matter. His mind kept slipping away.

With effort, he attempted to regain some ground. "Look, I'm sorry if—"

"No." Sasha pressed her finger against his lips, stopping him before he could say anything more. Before he could say something that hurt. "No 'sorry.' I'm not sorry," she told him softly. "And if you are, I don't want to hear about it. Not tonight. There're no strings attached, Tony. Just don't spoil it for me, that's all I ask." And then, because she could feel his desire for her growing, she allowed a smile to slip along her lips. "You can even have seconds if you want."

It was as if she'd read his mind. The spirit was willing, but the flesh was going to take a wee bit longer. "Give me a minute."

"I'll give you as long as you like," she told him. She lowered her eyes just a little. And smiled again. "But I don't think you'll need it."

And neither did he, he realized. His desire had taken full possession of him. Again. As he wove his fingers through her hair, his mouth curved in anticipation.

She was right. Tony had a heart-melting smile. Even a little went a long way. "You should do that more often."

He was just about to kiss her and stopped a fraction of an inch short of Sasha's lips. "What, make love with you?"

That, too, she thought. "I meant smile." Even a hint of one transformed his face, softening it. "You have a nice face." As if to underscore her words, she slid her hand along his cheek. She felt a muscle leap beneath her palm. Felt something tighten within her in response. "When you're not trying to scare people."

"I don't 'try' to scare people." He just went about business the only way he knew how. Doggedly.

"Right." She laughed quietly, the smile slipping into her eyes. And his gut. "It just comes naturally to you, I guess."

"You're not scared," he pointed out, his voice rumbling along her skin. Exciting her.

Slipping one hand beneath his head, she laced her hands around his neck. "Actually," she confessed, fitting her body against his, reveling in the heat that she felt emanating from his torso, "I'm terrified."

She couldn't help wondering if he realized that there was more than a little truth in her admission. Because she *was* afraid. Afraid of what she had just felt. Afraid of what she was feeling. She knew that, unlike with Adam, this couldn't lead anywhere. But somehow, she couldn't make herself pull back. Couldn't get herself to dive for shelter again. She was so weary of being numb. Of having a heart that pumped only blood and nothing more.

"I would have never guessed." But now that he looked into her eyes, there was something there, something that told him she wasn't merely being witty, or wry.

"I'm almost as good at hiding my feelings as you are."

She was striking too close. It was, he thought, bringing his mouth down to hers, as if she could look into his soul. Because, much as he tried to deny it, he was feeling something. And that scared the hell out of him.

Blocking out his thought, he focused only on the moment. Only on making love with Sasha again and nothing else.

The second time seemed even more intense, more pleasing, more of everything than the first had been. And it served to open his eyes even further.

He hadn't thought it was possible to feel this way again. To feel this surge through his veins, this need coursing through his body. He would have bet any amount of money that all of that had died for him the day that Annie had.

But here it was again, that wild, exhilarating feeling of being alive, of having things open up for him.

And yet, somehow, it was different.

He couldn't explain it, couldn't put his finger on it, but all Tony knew, dead center in his soul, was that it was different. Not better, not worse, than what he'd had with Annie, just different.

Damn it, don't analyze, just enjoy, he upbraided himself.

And so he did. Less urgently than before, because this time he allowed himself time to explore, to savor, to absorb and remember. Because he'd had one true love in his life and that was more than most. To think that he could get that lucky again would be taking up residence in a fool's paradise.

Spent, exhausted beyond words, Tony drew his body away from hers and tucked Sasha against him. He held her in silence, listening to the beat of her heart mimicking the rhythm of his own. He'd believed that moments like this were beyond his reach. To be allowed to revisit the peace, just this one more time, was something he was truly grateful for.

The next moment, peace flew out the window and adrenaline kicked in.

Someone was unlocking the front door.

Chapter 12

Tony bolted upright. Grabbing his jeans, he tossed his shirt at Sasha. He had his pants on and zipped before she had a chance to slip the shirt on.

"You expecting someone?"

"No."

The word was no sooner out of Sasha's mouth than the front door opened and a slender woman with auburn hair almost as vibrant as she was came in.

Sasha slanted a glance toward Tony. He amazed her. She'd never seen anyone get dressed so fast in her life. All she had managed to do was jam her arms into the shirtsleeves and close one strategic button before Natalya came walking in.

It could have been worse, Sasha thought. It could

have been her mother. She didn't even want to begin to think about the consequences if it had been her father.

"Lock's sticking again," Natalya complained. And then her mouth dropped open as she finally looked into the room. The key she'd been wrestling with was forgotten as it hung from the lock like a trapeze artist suspended in midair. Blinking to make sure her eyes weren't playing tricks on her, Natalya remained where she was, staring.

"Sasha?" she asked uncertainly.

Dragging a hand uncomfortably through his hair, Tony spoke first. "Let me take a look at that lock." Without waiting for an invitation, he padded barefoot over to the door.

And let me take a look at you, Natalya thought, her eyes slowly and appreciatively washing over the stranger's torso. This was certainly a much better specimen of manhood than she had just walked away from. When the latter had tried to hurry the evening into bed, she'd decided to cut short her plans for the weekend and come home.

She'd had no idea she'd be interrupting something. Sasha never brought men home.

Natalya sidestepped the handsome stranger as he came closer. "Um, Sash, there's a man in our apartment and he doesn't belong to either Kady or me."

Sasha took a deep breath. She was going to hear about this for weeks to come. Maybe months. "Yes, I know."

Natalya turned to the man, whose chest looked as if it had been chiseled out of rock and put out her hand. There was no attempt to hide the admiration in her eyes. "Hi, I'm Natalya, Sasha's sister."

"Anthony Santini," came the terse reply, coupled by an even terser handshake. He looked over her head toward Sasha. "Do you have any WD-40?"

"I'll get it," Natalya volunteered, glancing toward Sasha. The shirt her sister had on was hardly long enough to cover the bare essentials. "You don't look as if you're dressed for rummaging under the sink."

Natalya was back before Sasha could put on her own clothes. She'd had a chance to match the stranger's name with a scrap of information that had surfaced in her brain. Holding the small can out to him, Natalya said, "You're one of the police detectives investigating the murders at PM, aren't you?"

He took the can from her, then pulling a handkerchief out of his pocket, he held it around the wood surrounding the lock. Tony applied some of the spray before answering. "Yes."

Natalya glanced at her sister, then back at him. "Is this the way you usually question witnesses?" The woman's mouth, he noted, curved just the way that Sasha's did.

He squirted the spray into the lock a second time. "I was just getting ready to leave."

"Without your shirt?" Natalya asked innocently. She glanced toward Sasha, taking in the way her sister filled out the garment. "I don't think so." Finished,

Tony easily removed the key from the lock and tossed it to her. She caught them handily. "Take your time, Detective. There's this all-night deli that's just around the corner. I've got a sudden craving for a pastrami sandwich on rye. All things being equal, I should be gone for about an hour." She was already edging her way over to the door. "Longer if you need it."

"Natalya—" Sasha began to protest.

Natalya ignored her. "And be good to her," she added, opening the door. "Sasha doesn't do this kind of thing. Ever." Natalya paused to insert her key into the lock again, testing its mobility. "Perfect," she declared. Her eyes slid over his torso again as she stretched out the word. "I guess a little lubrication does do wonders." A mischievous smile curved her mouth just before she closed the door behind her.

Tony blew out a breath as he placed the can of WD-40 on the coffee table.

"Well, that was awkward." Sasha ran her hand through her hair. "I'm sorry. I didn't think she'd be home this weekend. Something must have happened," she realized. Sasha pressed her lips together. What was he thinking, she wondered. Was he angry at the interruption, or at being discovered in a compromising situation? His expression was unreadable. "Natalya tends to be a little outspoken. Sometimes she engages her mouth before her brain has had a chance to catch up. What she said about my not doing this sort of thing—"

"I already know that," he told her, his voice so low

she almost felt the words rather than heard them. His eyes held hers. "Neither do I."

So where did that put them? Sasha was afraid to ask. Afraid of the answer she might receive. Because she knew what she wanted to hear and knew that she would most likely hear the exact opposite. Better not to hear it said at all.

"Your sister was right about one thing," he finally said.

Sasha realized she was still holding her breath and let it out slowly. "And that was?"

Tony nodded toward her body. "I am going to need my shirt."

"What?" It took her a second to replay his words. And then she flushed, embarrassed. "Oh, right. Sure."

But before she could slip the shirt off and quickly put on the dress she'd shed earlier, Tony was doing it for her. He slowly slipped the shirt from her shoulders. But instead of putting it on or offering her the dress that had been discarded, he just stood there, his hands on her shoulders. She could have sworn that his breath had grown short. So had her own.

"Your sister said an hour?"

"Yes." Sasha could feel everything inside her begin to vibrate again as anticipation started to rise. Her reply was hardly more than a whisper.

"Does that mean an actual sixty minutes?" At this point, Tony wasn't taking anything for granted.

"Maybe more." Sasha drew her tongue along her lips. "Natalya has a tendency to run late."

"Good."

It was the last thing he said for a while.

The next time Natalya unlocked the apartment door, an hour and a half later, she did it with a great deal of commotion. She wanted to make sure that her re-entrance caught no one by surprise. Once the door had parted from the doorjamb, she stuck in a white handkerchief and waved it just for good measure.

Sasha was sitting on the sofa. The same sofa that had seen a great deal of activity in the last few hours. Seeing the white flag she laughed. "You can come in, Nat."

"The hunk is gone?" Opening the door all the way, Natalya looked around the living room, as if to see for herself.

"The hunk is gone," Sasha confirmed. She couldn't help the small, satisfied smile that escaped her lips. She slanted a look at her sister to see if she'd noticed. Natalya's wide grin told her she had. "What happened to your weekend?"

Natalya frowned, waving a dismissive hand. "Jerry's a jerk." And then her face brightened. "Tell me everything!"

In a flash, she crossed the room and grabbed both of Sasha's hands in hers, as if she intended to pump the story out of her if Sasha was unwilling to comply with her request.

Sasha laughed, disengaging herself from her sister. "You saw everything."

Natalya's grin turned from engaging to mischievous. Her eyes were sparkling.

"Not everything." A heartfelt sigh accompanied the words. "But from what I saw, this detective of yours was beautiful. So tell me," she said as she settled in for a lengthy story, "how long has this been going on?"

"He's not *my* detective," Sasha corrected. "And *this* has not been going on at all." She saw the impatient look on Natalya's face. Her sister clearly wasn't buying into this. She began to explain. "We were supposed to go out tonight for dinner—"

Natalya cut in, surprised. "Dinner? A date? And you didn't tell me?"

Sasha ignored the surprised accusation and pushed on to the conclusion of her short story. "But he was called away to another homicide. Except that he forgot to let me know that he wasn't coming to pick me up. So he came by later—to apologize."

Natalya whistled. "That man certainly knows how to offer up an apology." There was more than a touch of envy in her voice. "Can you get him to apologize again?"

"Natalya." There was a warning note in Sasha's voice, one that Natalya gave no indication she had even heard.

"Seriously," Natalya pushed on, "maybe you could offer to help him with his investigation and when he snaps at you—he looks like the snapping type—" she confided, "he'll feel guilty and apologize again." Natalya sighed, thinking of what she'd almost walked in on. "Does he have any brothers who like to apologize—?"

Sasha knew that Natalya could go on like this indefinitely. She didn't want a big deal being made of what had just happened, even if Tony was the first man she'd been with since Adam. It would all soon be in her past. The best way to stop her sister was a cold dose of reality.

"Natalya, Tyler Harris is dead."

"Tyler Harris?" Skidding to a verbal halt, Natalya then repeated the name slowly. "Tyler Harris?" She was drawing a blank and shook her head, looking at Sasha for enlightenment.

"He's an anesthesiologist, or was," Sasha amended. God, but she was having trouble accepting all this as being real. She kept hoping it was all a nightmare and that she'd wake up. "Tyler used to work at PM." Even as she said the words, something came back to her. A wisp of a memory that went through her fingers like smoke when she tried to catch it.

"Sasha? What's the matter?" Natalya asked, concerned. "You look pale."

And then it came to her. Not a fragment but the entire scenario. Her eyes widened with surprise as she looked at her sister. Why hadn't she remembered earlier?

"Tyler and I once were in the O.R. together. It was the Sunday after Thanksgiving and there was almost no one in the E.R." As more bits and pieces returned to attach themselves to the memory, her voice began to grow progressively more agitated. "The EMTs brought in a woman who'd been in a hit-and-run car accident. Tyler administered the anesthesia and I operated. There wasn't time to get a specialist." She hadn't thought about that in a long time, had put the entire incident in the back of her mind because the results had not been good. Despite all her best efforts, the woman had died on the table.

Died. The single word vibrated in her brain. Her eyes widened.

Omigod.

She became aware of Natalya's hand on her arm. "Sasha? Sasha, what's wrong? You look as if you'd seen a ghost."

She had. A ghost from the past. She looked at Natalya. "Angela and Rachel were the nurses in the O.R. that day. We were short-staffed. The woman's body was a mess. I couldn't find the source of her internal bleeding. I sent Jorge to get more blood…" Her voice trailed off. "I sent Jorge," she repeated. "Jorge was there."

Everyone she'd just mentioned was dead.

Except for her.

A cold, clammy feeling descended over her.

And then, through the haze that had suddenly enshrouded her, she heard Natalya's voice. "Are you trying to tell me that everyone who was in the O.R. with you that day has been killed by that psycho who is stalking PM?"

Spoken out loud, that sounded absurd. Sasha let out a long breath. She was letting her imagination run away with her.

Sasha shook her head in response to Natalya's question. "Maybe it's a coincidence."

But Natalya was far from convinced. She shook her head grimly. "You don't believe in coincidences, Sasha. Remember? And neither do I."

She was about to protest that a coincidence was more likely than the scenario she'd just mentioned, but then another thought came to her. A horrifying thought. She looked at Natalya.

"Oh my God, Joshua."

"Joshua?" Natalya repeated, confused. She narrowed her eyes, trying to fathom what her sister was telling her. Sasha had her hand on her wrist and was squeezing. Hard.

"Joshua Palmer," she cried. If this outrageous thought had any merit to it, the young physician could be next. "He was the assistant at the surgery." Natalya said nothing, continuing to listen. "He's a primary-care physician, Nat, specializing in internal organs. We thought, between the two of us, we could keep the injured woman alive until Norman Fernandez could be located and answered his page."

"Anyone else in the operating room?" Natalya wanted to know.

Sasha shook her head. "No. Just the five of us. And Jorge."

"Six, with four dead," Natalya reviewed, no

longer smiling. No longer thinking about the scene she'd just walked in on. "Sasha, you've got to tell your hunk about this."

Sasha was already striding across the floor to the phone on the coffee table. More than anything else, she hoped she was wrong, that this really was just a bizarre coincidence. "I already told you, Nat. He's not my hunk."

Natalya joined her at the telephone. "Then I'd let him down easy, because I think he thinks he is." And she meant that, seriously. "And I wouldn't tell him until after this psycho stalker, whoever he is, is caught. You're going to definitely need that sexy detective for protection."

Sasha began to protest, then fell silent as she heard the phone on the other end of the line begin to ring. She waved her hand at Natalya, indicating that she should hold her tongue.

A deep, sleepy voice muttered, "Santini."

She immediately felt guilty and would have hung up had Natalya not been right there at her side, watching. So she pushed on, telling herself that she was right to call. "Did I wake you?"

She heard Tony let out a long breath, as if he was getting his bearings. And putting a lid on his temper. He didn't answer her question.

Instead, he responded to what he heard in her voice. "Something wrong, Doc?"

So, they were back to that. To their job descriptions. She'd hoped they had moved beyond that. But then, she reminded herself, she had known going into this that he was the type who wanted to maintain his distance.

"It might be," she began slowly, trying hard to sound as if she was rational. "I'm not sure, but I think I might have found your connection between the dead people."

"I'm listening."

She could detect a note of electricity crackling between the lines. She'd gotten his undivided attention.

"Three years ago, on the Sunday after Thanksgiving, we all operated on a hit-and-run victim." She enunciated every word as if she as waiting for him to absorb them one at a time.

"Hold it, hold it," he ordered gruffly. He was certain his foggy brain had caused him to mishear her. Or at least he fervently hoped so. "You said 'we.' Is that a royal 'we'?"

Sasha took a breath before answering. That meant that she was in danger, too, didn't it? She refused to allow her mind to go there, to deal with that thought.

"No, it's not a royal 'we', Detective. I was there, too. It was a hit-and-run," she said again with emphasis. "The paramedics brought her in, a young woman about twenty-five years old. There was no one on duty that night who specialized in internal surgery. If we'd waited until a specialist arrived, there was a hundred percent chance she would be dead before the surgeon ever crossed the threshold." Sasha paused.

"Did you save her?" Tony asked the question for form's sake. He had a feeling that he already knew the answer.

The next moment, she confirmed it. "No, she died while we were operating." Sasha sighed, remembering. Feeling helpless and awful. The woman had been young. And three months pregnant.

He heard the sadness in her voice and ignored the urge to say something to comfort her. There were more important things at stake right now. There was nothing to be gained by feeling guilty about the woman's death. It wouldn't change the results. He was certain that Sasha had done all that had been humanly possible. At the moment, he was far more interested in keeping her and whoever else had been involved in that emergency surgery alive.

"Can you remember if the woman was married or about to be married?"

Sasha heard rustling on the other side of the line, as if Tony was moving around, getting dressed. She tried not to allow herself to get distracted by that thought, by the image of him slipping into clothes the way he had done earlier.

Instead, she concentrated on his question. On the memory of an operation that was three years in the past. "Yes, she was. Her husband threatened to sue everyone." She remembered that the man had been angry and abusive to her when she came out to break the news to him. She'd had the woman's blood on her surgical livery and it had nearly sent him over the edge. "But in the end," she said, struggling to regain her calm, "the whole thing just blew over."

Tony had a different view of it. "Maybe not. I'll be right down there. In the meantime, try to remember as much as you can about the operation, who was there, what the husband might have said, things like that."

"You don't need to come rushing over, Tony," she protested.

Maybe they weren't back to square one after all, he thought. That should have bothered him, he told himself. But the exact opposite was true. "Is your sister back yet?" he wanted to know.

Sasha glanced at Natalya, who'd remained only a couple of feet away from her during the entire phone call. Maybe he wasn't worried about her. Maybe, since she'd woken him, he'd decided to come back for an encore. She could feel tiny nerve endings priming, sending off alarms. "Yes, but—"

"Good. Keep the door locked and don't let anyone else in until I get there."

He *was* worried. She could feel her uneasiness increasing even as she silently insisted she was making something out of nothing. "I might be all wrong about this."

"And then again, you might be all right," he countered grimly. "Keep the door locked."

Ten minutes later, he was there, banging on her door and calling through it for her to let him in.

Sasha all but flew to the door, taking the chain off even as she flipped the lock.

"I didn't realize you lived so close by."

"I don't," he told her, crossing the threshold. Turning, he closed the door and secured the chain. "One of the advantages of having a police siren in your car is that you get to use it once in a while to prevent crimes instead of getting there after the fact." He nodded at Natalya, but his attention was completely centered on Sasha. "Was there anyone else in the operating room that night?"

She'd thought and rethought that surgery the minute they hung up the phone. "Just Joshua Palmer. He's a primary-care physician."

Tony frowned. He hated the labels that society had slapped on everything. He missed the days when a doctor like Palmer was simply referred to as a family physician and that was enough to speak volumes.

"Anyone else?" he wanted to know. Sasha shook her head. "And everyone who's been killed so far," he repeated the names of all four victims slowly, "Angela Rico, Rachel Wells, Jorge Lopez and Tyler Harris, they were all in the operating room that night, too?"

Sasha was beginning to feel hollow inside. And extremely uneasy. "Yes."

"Can you remember the woman's name?"

That she wasn't liable to forget any time soon, Sasha thought. She nodded as she pressed her lips together. "You tend to remember the one you lose, no matter how hard you try to forget them. Her name was Gloria Jean Anderson."

The first order of business, Tony thought, after calling the captain and getting authorization for Sasha and the other doctor to have bodyguards posted, was having a talk with the late Gloria Jean's husband.

It felt good to finally have some kind of lead to work with. He nodded at Sasha as he took out his cell phone. "It's going to be all right."

The optimistic promise surprised her.

Chapter 13

"Dr. Pulaski, have you seen the paper this morning?"

The breathless question came from one of the newest nurses on the floor, Jennifer Cruz, as Sasha was quickly walking past the nurses' station on the maternity ward the following morning.

It was a little before nine and she was running behind. She always did her rounds at the hospital before going to her office. Today, mercifully, was a light day. Only three of the patients on the floor were hers, and one was going home this morning as soon as she signed the discharge papers.

Without looking, Sasha had a feeling she knew what Jennifer was referring to. "No, I didn't have time." She glanced toward the nurse. "I'm running late. Oh God." The groan was an involuntary reaction to the headline that was splashed across the first page of the newspaper that the nurse was holding up for her to view. "Hospital Stalker Strikes Again." The headline fairly vibrated. Sasha sighed. It didn't take the media long. "Just what we need. More panicked patients."

Sasha saw the animation drain away from the nurse's face. The next moment, she discovered why.

"The medical staff isn't feeling too good about this killer being at large, either," Lauren James complained.

The administrator came up behind her. The woman looked slightly harried beneath her perfectly made-up features. The board, Sasha knew, was not taking this well. Which meant that they were, in turn, taking it out on Lauren.

Despite the differences they'd had, Sasha felt sorry for the woman.

"Everyone's looking over their shoulder. Patients are canceling elective surgeries, or postponing them." For a moment, Lauren paused, as if debating her next words. It was a known fact that the woman had no friends. Up until now, Sasha would have said that Lauren felt she didn't need them. But now, judging by the look on Lauren's face, she wasn't so sure. "The board is threatening to have my head."

Though she felt certain that the board was not happy about this unwanted publicity the hospital was getting, she had a feeling that the members were using the fallout as an excuse to make Lauren's life difficult. Difficult enough perhaps to make the woman hand in her resignation of her own accord. It was no secret that, education and credentials notwithstanding, the woman was no one's candidate for hospital administrator of the year. Or even the month.

Still, Sasha felt obligated to lend a sympathetic ear. "They can't blame you for these murders."

Lauren had purposely moved away from the nurses' station and Jenny's rather unsubtle attempt to listen in. She kept her voice low as she said, "Tell that to the board."

"Well, unless you're responsible for killing these people—and everyone knows how you hate to get your hands dirty," Sasha quipped with a wry smile, "there's really no way that you could be behind this."

The icy blonde shrugged her shoulders as her lips curled into a deep frown. And then her eyes seemed to grow alert as she looked over Sasha's shoulder. "Who's that?" she wanted to know.

Sasha turned to look. Lauren was referring to a man not more than several paces away. To the casual observer it was obvious that the stranger didn't look like either an anxious husband or a happy one.

She'd told Tony the man didn't blend in, Sasha thought, frustrated. She'd left the apartment quickly this morning, hoping to ditch the detective assigned to her. She should have known better.

"My police protection," Sasha told Lauren.

This was not going to work. Harry Ackerman had been introduced to her last night. Last night, she'd assumed that the detective would be outside her apartment, in his car, unobtrusively standing guard. It wasn't just herself needing protecting last night.

But today, it was a whole different story. Today the detective would only be getting in her way. And she couldn't have that. Her first allegiance was to her patients.

"You have police protection?" Lauren looked at her, stunned. "Why? What else has happened?" she wanted to know.

But Sasha ignored the questions as she crossed over to the dour, slightly rumpled-looking man. He towered over her by almost a foot. He hadn't been picked for his ability to blend in, she thought.

"Look, Detective Ackerman, I'm sorry but this just isn't going to work. No offense, but having you around is going to get my patients nervous. Not to mention that I've got exams to perform." She looked up at him pointedly. "And you can't be present."

"It's Harry," he told her. Willing to work within the situation he said, "Then I'll be in the reception area."

She took a breath, knowing this was going to make her seem as if she were being difficult, but that wasn't her intent. "Can I refuse police protection, Harry?"

"Yes," he allowed, saying the word slowly. "But I don't recommend it."

It wasn't his place to recommend that he not be around, she thought. Especially since Tony had gone through channels to obtain his services. But if she'd found the idea of having protection comforting last night, in the light of day, she knew that her own fears had to take second place to her patients' needs.

"Duly noted, Harry. And it's not that I don't appreciate it, I do. But I have to officially refuse protection." She offered the older man an apologetic smile. "Tell Detective Santini thanks but no thanks."

"He's not going to be happy about this," Ackerman warned her.

That she already knew. Santini was a headstrong man. But she was well acquainted with headstrong.

"You're sending the police detective away?" Lauren was still trying to fathom what was going on in her hospital.

Sasha nodded. Returning to the nurses' station, she went to the main desk and pulled a chart. "It wouldn't work out."

"You didn't answer me before," Lauren reminded her. She rephrased her question. "Why do you merit special police protection while the rest of the hospital staff doesn't? Is there something I should know?" Suspicion was all over her face.

More than anything else, Lauren James hated being out of the loop. About *anything*. Annoyance creased her brow, creating tiny furrows of disapproval. Had she been of a different temperament, Sasha would have played the moment out for a while for her own amusement. But there was nothing to be gained by that.

So she told Lauren, even though she knew she was probably opening up a can of worms. "Because the investigating detective thinks there's a connection between me and the four victims, including the latest one." She nodded toward the newspaper.

"A connection?" Lauren echoed, clearly horrified. "What kind of a connection?"

"We all worked on a hit-and-run patient three years ago. She died on the operating table. I was the surgeon, Tyler was the anesthesiologist. Joshua Palmer was the assistant."

"Three years," Lauren repeated. "That was before I came to Patience Memorial."

And glorious times they were, too, Sasha thought, although her expression never changed. "Yes, I know. At the time I'd only been here, as an attending, for six months."

Making a notation in the chart, she closed it and placed it back on the desk. Ackerman, she noticed, was still lingering in the corridor, uncertain as to whether or not he should leave.

As she came out of the nurses' station, Sasha made eye contact with him. "Really, go," she urged. "If there's any heat, I'll take it. Tell Detective Santini it was my doing, my choice."

With that, she put the matter of killings and stalkers out of her mind and walked into the first room. She had patients to attend to and that came before anything.

"So," Sasha said cheerfully, addressing the woman in the hospital bed, "are you and your beautiful daughter ready to go home, Sandy?"

"The guy's alibi checks out." It was the second time Henderson had said the sentence to Tony. There was still no response from the man. Henderson leaned over his partner's desk, peering at his face. "Santini, did you hear me? Gloria Jean Anderson's husband, his—"

Tony waved a hand at his partner. He and Henderson had brought Anderson in for questioning first thing that morning. The college professor's haughty attitude had made it a case of instant dislike on his part. He'd grilled the man intently, getting his whereabouts for the time of death for all four victims.

The alibis hadn't been creative, but they'd obviously been genuine. Henderson had been checking them out for the remainder of the morning.

"Yeah, I heard you," Tony grumbled. "I just didn't want to hear you."

Henderson blew out an audible breath, leaning against the side of Tony's desk.

"Yeah, I know what you mean." He shook his head. "It really looked like you were onto something there. But the guy was in Vegas for the first killing. And at some seminar for the college for the second. He was giving a lecture when Harris was killed. Lots of people saw him all those times." Henderson flipped the pages of his small, battered notepad, as if he expected something magical to pop up, something that hadn't been there all the other times he'd opened the notepad. With a helpless shrug, he tucked it back into the pocket of his hound's-tooth jacket. "Maybe there's something else that ties all those victims together. You came up with one operation, maybe there's another. It's a busy hospital."

He hadn't come up with the operation. Sasha had. He would have liked nothing better than to take her out of the equation. Except that his gut told him she belonged in it. And that she was right about this.

Tony didn't liked the late Gloria Jean Anderson's husband. A tall, rangy man with dirty blond hair, condescending brown eyes and a nasty disposition that had flared once he'd discovered he was being approached by a member of the police. An English professor who had no qualms about showing that he felt superior to everyone he spoke to, Simon Anderson blamed the entire police force for never apprehending the hit-and-run driver responsible for his wife's death.

A little delving into records showed that Simon and his late wife had had marital problems. The counsellor they'd gone to see had recommended Simon sign up for anger-management classes. The man had attended one class before dropping out.

It took very little effort for Tony to envision Anderson plotting and exacting revenge for his wife's death. Since he couldn't find the hit-and-run driver, wiping out the medical team who had failed to save her would have undoubtedly been a close second.

Except that he had alibis. Or so it looked on the surface, Tony thought.

"Maybe," he agreed. "Why don't you dig a little deeper, make sure that our boy didn't hire someone to do his dirty work. Check into his finances, see if any large sum of money moved out of his accounts recently. Hit men don't come cheap. Maybe—" Tony stopped abruptly as he saw Harry Ackerman walking into the squad room.

Leaving his thought, and Henderson, hanging, Tony got out of his chair and crossed over to the detective. The latter obviously hadn't seen him and was walking to the rear of the squad room, to the captain's office.

"Hey, Ackerman," Tony called. "What's up? Why aren't you with Dr. Pulaski?" And then a partial answer occurred to him. His expression drew deadly serious. "Something happen?"

Ackerman stopped walking. He frowned. The jowls on his face resembled that of a well-fed hound dog. "Yeah, something happened. The doc told me to tell you that she's decided to refuse police protection."

"What?" That was a stupid move and Sasha did not strike him as a stupid woman.

"She told me to tell you she's decided to refuse police protection," Ackerman repeated a little more slowly. He knew better than to flippantly ask Santini if he was going deaf.

Tony waved an impatient hand at Ackerman. He could feel Henderson staring at him. It just served to heighten his annoyance. What the hell was going on here? Why would the woman suddenly decide to play hero?

"I heard you the first time." His eyes narrowed as he looked at Ackerman. "What did you do to make her change her mind?"

Ackerman straightened, like a man bracing himself for a blow. "Nothing."

"You must have done something," Tony insisted, doing his best not to lose his temper. He'd never been on the easygoing side but lately it felt as if all his emotions were closer to the surface than they'd ever been. Ready to explode. "Everything was all right last night when I left you there outside her apartment."

Ackerman moved his wide shoulders in a hapless shrug. "Don't look at me. It wasn't my idea. She said I scared her patients. I offered to stay in her reception area, but she didn't think that was good enough, or far enough away," he added, annoyed himself.

The man wasn't exactly warm and cuddly, but he wasn't Frankenstein either, Tony thought in exasperation. Pulling out his cell phone, he punched in Sasha's number. He listened to the phone ring five times before her voice came on. But as he began to speak, he realized he was talking to a pre-recorded message.

Tony bit off a curse as he waited for the beep as instructed.

"Listen," he said into the phone after the beep had sounded, trying to ignore the fact that he was conversing with a machine, something he hated, "you don't get to call off police protection. Only *I* get to do that. Damn it, I hate talking to machines," he shouted.

It was the last thing he said into the phone before terminating the call.

When Tony started striding through the squad room, heading toward the exit, Henderson was quick to follow. He was only a step behind the primary investigator as they walked out into the corridor.

"Okay, so what's the plan, Santini?" he wanted to know.

The plan. He hadn't anything as clear-cut as a plan. He was back to flying by the seat of his pants—and following his gut. And his gut told him that Sasha might be the next target.

"I'm going back to the hospital. The key to all these murders has to be there. Maybe I can get the administrator to have one of her people cross-reference all the patient records against the staff they interacted with." If the woman refused because of some doctor-patient privilege, he had a few other options to try that weren't quite so much on the straight and narrow. But he'd learned to give protocol a try whenever possible. "Maybe there's a connection there."

"No more bodyguards?" Henderson wanted to know.

"I didn't say that," Tony bit off. His tone told Henderson to back off.

Henderson was very good at picking up on tones. It was part of the secret of his longevity on the force— and why he'd managed to survive for as long as he had with Tony. He knew better than to rock the boat.

"No, no, Dad, I'm okay. We're all okay. You don't have to come out of retirement. Really," Sasha insisted. The second she'd seen the story on Tyler Harris's murder, she'd been expecting her father's call. She'd already had one from her mother.

She was beginning to think of the cell phone as an evil invention, meant to bedevil her.

"I have already made up my mind, Sasha. Conrad has been after me to join the security firm he is running. Now I have a reason."

Conrad Zemanski was her father's oldest and best friend. Both had served on the police force together. Conrad had taken early retirement after having been wounded on the job. A small inheritance from his wife's uncle had given him enough money to start his own security firm. A firm her father seemed dead set on joining now.

"Daddy, even if you do become a guard, that doesn't mean that you'll automatically be sent over to PM. Conrad might not even have a contract with the hospital." She crossed her fingers as she said it.

"Yes, he does," her father's voice boomed in her ear. "Conrad's firm has a contract with many of the hospitals in the area. I told him what was happening, and your hospital is looking for more security even as we are talking."

Sasha closed her eyes, searching for strength. "Daddy, you don't have to do this. Detective Santini's already assigned a bodyguard to me." *And I got rid of him, but you don't have to know that.*

"Why? Why just you? What is it you are not telling me?"

She realized her mistake too late. "I always tell you everything, Daddy. And I'm not the only one getting a bodyguard. There're several other doctors as well." It was a white lie, but under the circumstances, she could be forgiven, she thought. She was only out to give her parents peace of mind. Instead of losing her own. "So you see, I'm fine. You can stop worrying." The sun, she knew, would stop rising sooner than her father would stop worrying, but she was bound to go through the motions.

"Sasha, you know that I—"

She could smell an argument coming. "I've got to go, Daddy. I'm being paged. Oops, that's Mrs. Miller. Twins," she told him hurriedly. "Babies don't wait to be born. Love to Mom."

She disconnected the call before he had a chance to make another protest or mount another argument. With a sigh, she leaned back in her chair, eyes closed.

"It's not nice to lie to your father."

Startled, Sasha swung her chair around to face the doorway. Her pulse accelerated when she saw Tony standing there. She drew in a long breath to steady it, hoping that she hadn't suddenly become flushed. Flushed was for teenagers. Not even teenagers, she amended.

She watched Tony enter the room. It was more as though he took possession of it. "What are you doing here?"

His expression was unreadable. "Listening to you lie to your father."

She straightened her shoulders defensively. "I wasn't lying."

"Oh?" Crossing his arms before him, he leaned a hip against her desk. Parking his torso much too close to her. "What do you call untruths in your world?"

"I call it making him feel better." She loved her father, but he was the poster child for the overprotective dad. "If he had his way, my sisters and I would all be wrapped up in cotton batting and stored in some large closet."

"The man was a cop," Tony reminded her. He felt a smile attempting to curve his lips. She had that effect on him, he thought as he banked it down. "He knows better than most what could happen."

"All of life's a risk. By definition," Sasha added with emphasis. She deflected the conversation back toward him. "Now, what are you really doing here?"

The smile faded on its own. "Why did you send Ackerman away?"

"I told him why. I can't do my work and have him looking over my shoulder. My patients expect privacy and rightly so."

She was smarter than that, he thought. Ackerman wasn't going to be standing two inches away from her while she was in her office. He was supposed to provide protection for her as she went from one place to another.

"He'd keep out of your way," he told her.

A good number of her patients were pregnant right now. Which meant that their hormones and emotions were in flux. It didn't help to see a hulking man sitting in the waiting room.

"None of my patients are going to suddenly pull out a gun on me."

"No." He did his best to keep his temper, but there was no denying that he was wasting time trying to convince her of something that he felt was necessary. "But someone else might."

She didn't want to think about that. "Did you check out the husband?"

Tony nodded. "He's clean. Nasty son of a bitch, but clean."

She smiled, storing her frustration for a moment as she touched his face.

Sasha felt stirrings. Too fast, too intense. She dropped her hand, needing to get a handle on this before it overwhelmed her.

"Maybe it was just a coincidence, all the victims being in the O.R. with that patient." She shrugged ruefully. "My fault for thinking there was something to it."

They both thought there was something to it. "I don't believe in coincidences."

"But if the husband's clean…"

"Maybe we didn't dig deep enough," he countered. He surprised himself by letting her into his thought process. "You remember ever being in the O.R. with them on any other occasion?"

She shook her head. "No. We interacted, saw each other in the halls, but our fields of expertise didn't bring us into the O.R. together—except for that one occasion."

"I've got Henderson at the hospital, having Lauren James dig into the records, cross-referencing them to see if the victims ever had any joint dealings with any other patient. You might not even figure into the equation," he added.

Her eyes met his. He didn't really believe that, she thought. But for the sake of argument, she said, "Then I really won't be needing police protection."

Tony looked at her for a long moment. "Don't be so quick to refuse police protection."

"Do I get to choose which detective I have protecting me?" she said playfully.

She already had the answer to that, he thought. "I'll be by later to take you home. You'll be here?"

"Here or at the hospital."

"You'll be here."

This time, it wasn't a question. It was an order. She felt herself bristling slightly. And then the buzzer on her telephone went off. "That's Lisa," she told him, referring to her nurse. "She gets on my case if I start falling behind."

"I'll let you get back to your work," he told her, crossing to the threshold. He paused for a moment longer. "Don't leave without me."

The order made her feel simultaneously protected, rebellious—and nervous. For a whole barrage of reasons.

Chapter 14

Tony finally got Sasha to agree to let him bring her home when she was finished. And then he was faced with waiting for her day to end. He discovered that she actually kept worse hours than he did.

Long after his own workday was officially closed—and for once, there were no calls on his cell—she was still on the job. The moment he finished the last of his paperwork at the precinct, he called Sasha to make sure she was still at her office. It wasn't that he didn't trust her, but he'd learned in a very short matter of time that the woman was unbelievably headstrong. Willful even as she flashed that innocent smile at him.

Lisa had left for the day and Sasha answered her

own phone, just in case it was one of the mothers-to-be. Her voice grew warm and intimate the moment she recognized his voice.

"I'm just heading out to the hospital to make my rounds before I go home," she told him. "Barring an emergency, I should be done in about half an hour or so."

"Wait for me," he instructed.

She could hear movement on the other end of the line and could almost see him slipping on his jacket, heading for the door. Trying to outrun her.

Sasha smiled. "Tony, I am perfectly capable of crossing the street and walking into the hospital on my own."

He knew she'd say that. Knew, too, that it was useless to argue with her. She'd do what she wanted to do. All he could hope for was compromise. "Don't take any shortcuts."

He heard the smile in her voice and could envision her giving a mock salute. "Yes, sir, Detective, sir. Only long cuts."

He wondered if she actually thought this was a joke, or if she was doing this for his benefit. "In plain sight, Sasha."

"Does Dr. Palmer get this kind of up-close-and-personal service?" she wanted to know.

"No."

"Why?" she teased.

There was a long pause on the line before she heard him say in a low whisper that fairly raised goose bumps on her flesh, "I haven't slept with Dr. Palmer."

"Good to know. See you at the hospital." With that, she broke the connection.

She'd made a joke in response to his answer because the implications of his words might have been serious. The trouble was, she *wanted* them to be serious. But she couldn't afford to go there just in case they weren't. Just in case he was only talking and nothing more.

Sasha sighed as she went down in the elevator. She didn't want to open up her heart and risk having it snatched out of her chest again. Loving a man had taken its toll on her, had had its price. Allowing love to take her prisoner again, well, she didn't know if she was up to that.

As if she had a choice, she thought ruefully, hurrying across the street to the hospital entrance.

Love, her mother had once told her, although not in these exact words, was not like a faucet that you could turn off and on. It happened of its own accord and you could chose to follow your heart or not, but you couldn't dictate who you did or didn't love. It just wasn't that easy.

And nothing about Detective Tony Santini was easy, she thought later that night as he brought her not just into her building, but to her apartment door. The man would have made the word *hello* difficult.

She paused at her door just before she began the search for her key. "Would you like to come in?"

More than you'll ever know, he thought. And his professional responsibility had nothing to do with it. Interwoven into his investigation, into all the reams of facts and databases he'd gone through, had been thoughts of this dark-haired, blue-eyed doctor. Of the night they'd spent together. Of the nights to come that he wanted to spend with her.

This wasn't like him, he berated himself. He had ironclad control over his feelings, over his thoughts.

Or at least he had had.

Until he'd taken on this case. And her.

He shrugged at her invitation, trying to appear indifferent. Trying, without success, to maintain a professional relationship. "I thought I'd just, you know, stay in the car for the night."

It was downright cold tonight. He'd freeze sitting in his car and he couldn't leave the heater on all night. The fact that he didn't want to remain in her apartment told her that maybe she'd misinterpreted the signals he'd been sending.

She looked up into his eyes. Trying not to get lost. "I thought we decided that I don't need a body-guard."

He shook his head in response. "No, you decided you didn't want someone looking over your shoulder while you worked. There were no actual decisions made about you not having a bodyguard."

She made one more attempt to bow out gracefully. "I'm safe," she insisted. He raised one eyebrow, obviously waiting to hear what led her to this conclusion. "My sisters are probably in the apartment. The murderer only kills his victims, no collateral damage."

"So far," Tony was quick to point out, his tone indicating that it was just a matter of time. "Our boy's not a serial killer, he's a dedicated executioner. We're not dealing with an obsessive-compulsive. He could easily change his pattern just to get what he's after." He pinned her with a penetrating look that went clear back to her spine. "You want to take that chance with your sisters' lives?"

He knew he had her there.

"If you're going to be my bodyguard, then you can stay in the apartment." She raised her chin. Her breath skimmed along his skin. "Closer to the body you're supposed to be guarding."

He found himself only an inch away from her. And wanting even that distance to melt away. Tony felt his belly tighten. "How close?"

She smiled at him, knowing she was going to regret this in the morning. Or the next morning. Or the morning after that. But right now, she didn't have enough willpower to push him away. To hold herself in check. Nor did she really want any.

"As close as you like."

He knew how close he'd like. But that would require his putting his very job description on hold and he just couldn't afford to get distracted. Her life might depend on it.

Besides, her sisters were inside the apartment and

he wasn't one of those people who could block out the world and allow himself to indulge in his fantasy. But, if he were being honest with himself, he'd been blocking out the world, standing on the outside, for most of his life.

There was a war going on inside of him and no matter which side won, he'd lose.

Framing Sasha's delicate face with his hands, he brought her mouth closer to his and then he kissed her. Slowly. As if they had all the time in the world instead of a finite amount, after which he would return to his duties, his world, and she would go back to hers.

But the kiss satisfied nothing.

It only made him want more. Made him want her more. So much that he felt desire become almost overwhelming in proportion.

The kiss deepened, taking him on an exhilarating ride that demanded more. He could almost hear a small voice in his head crying: *Again!*

Her arms were around his neck, her body pressed close to his. So close that the coat she was wearing and the jacket he had on seemed to burn away at the first sign of contact.

She didn't want this to stop. She wanted to make love with Tony again. Here, now, in the hall, it didn't matter where as long as it happened.

Quickly.

Where had her common sense gone? Her restraint? Her grasp of decorum?

All of it seemed to have burned at the very first

contact of his mouth to hers. It was as if her very body was on fire. She needed to feel his hands on her. To feel them skimming along her curves.

To feel his body, his skin, hot and hard, against hers.

Sasha moaned as the kiss made her head spin and her breathing become labored. She didn't want this to end. Not yet. She needed to store up the wild, erratic emotion coursing through her veins. Store it up for when there would be nothing again.

It took them both a second to realize that the door to the apartment had opened.

Tony was the first to sense the difference, to feel the slight shift of air that indicated the change of surroundings. Pulling back from Sasha, his hand flew to the hilt of his weapon in a motion that defied visual verification. One second he was holding her, the next, he had his gun out and trained on the opened doorway.

Natalya swallowed a squeal, her initial reaction to seeing the drawn weapon. Instead, she quipped, "Get a room, you two." There was no denying that she'd been waiting for the sound of Sasha's return. This stalker business had all of them nervous. "Preferably Sasha's," she told Tony, then nodded at the weapon. "Or a firing range if you'd feel more comfortable."

Tony holstered his firearm. He wondered if Sasha's sister knew how close she'd come to needing medical attention.

"Sorry," he murmured. "You move too quietly."

"Maybe you were too busy to hear me." And then Natalya looked at the gun that was now safely holstered. "And then again, maybe not." She shifted her attention to Sasha. "You're late. Call next time."

"Since when?" Sasha wanted to know.

They never called one another to say that they were going to be extra late. It was understood that erratic hours went with the territory. That was one of the reasons they had all moved in together instead of remaining in their parents' house in Queens—the freedom to come and go as they needed to with no explanations. The close proximity to the hospital was just an added bonus.

For once, Natalya's expression was very serious. "Since you started being stalked."

"There's still no indication of that," Sasha was quick to remind her. "The fact that we'd all worked together that one time could just be a coincidence, especially since that woman's husband can't be connected to any of the killings."

Tony found himself exchanging looks with Natalya. He realized that Sasha's sister didn't believe in coincidences either. But for the time being, he let Sasha's protest go. He walked into the apartment after Sasha.

Sasha paused to close the door. Out of the corner of her eye, she saw Tony slip the chain into place. "Tony's staying the night," she told her sister.

Natalya nodded, as if to say it was about time. "Good."

"In an official capacity," Tony felt compelled to clarify.

At that, Natalya's serious expression vanished. "Hey, whatever rings your chimes," she said. "Me, I'm catching up on my favorite show thanks to the magic of VHS recording and then going to bed." She flashed a wicked smile at Tony. "I'm a very sound sleeper," she confided.

"I'll be on the couch," Tony responded.

Natalya's grin grew larger. The look in her eyes said she didn't believe him for a minute.

"Of course you will." She paused to look at Sasha before going to her room and the wide-screen TV she'd treated herself to. "G'night."

"Where's Kady?" Sasha called after her. There was no light coming from beneath Kady's door to indicate that she was home. And Sasha felt certain her sister would have come out to join in the second she'd heard voices in the living room.

"At PM. She just got called down about twenty minutes ago. One of her patients had a minor Transient Ischemic Attack. Nothing serious, but the man's wife wanted Kady to check him out." There was an unmistakable touch of pride in her voice as she added, "Wouldn't let anyone else touch him. Well, good night again. Happy guarding, Detective," she said with as straight a face as she could manage. And then she was gone.

Sasha turned away from the hall and saw that Tony had walked over to the sofa. He looked about to plant himself there for the duration of the night. She knew he'd remain there, too, unless she said something.

"You know," Sasha began innocently, "if guarding me is your intent, you could probably do a better job if you were closer."

He wasn't the kind who was schooled in the games that men and women played. But he knew an invitation when he heard one. It took him less than thirty seconds to debate the merits of remaining on the sofa or of staying in her room. It really wasn't much of a contest.

"You might have a point," he allowed, rising to his feet.

Sasha laughed. "I'm the doctor. I *always* have a point." She held out her hand to him.

The next moment, Tony laced his fingers with hers and allowed Sasha to lead him to her room. Where he guarded her. Up close and very personal.

Leaving the delivery room, Sasha wiped her brow with the side of her forearm. She was exhausted. Not as exhausted as Edie Wilson, she was willing to bet, but still pretty exhausted.

Edie Wilson had gone into labor at 6:32 a.m. when her water had broken as she was getting out of bed. This was her first baby and she panicked. Her husband, Miles, broke all the speed postings and got to the hospital in record time, leaving more than a few drivers, she was willing to bet, cursing in his wake. He needn't have bothered hurrying, because Edie's labor went on and on. And on.

With each hour that went by, the frustration and the pain seemed to grow, as did Edie's feelings of hopelessness. Sasha had attended her first thing this morning. But after an hour and a half, when it appeared that Baby Wilson was not about to make an appearance any time soon, Sasha had gone to her office—only after swearing that she would check in on Edie at regular intervals.

The hospital, she'd reminded Edie, was only five minutes from the office by foot. Three if those feet were running.

At six that evening, with Edie's screams ringing in her ears, Sasha made a decision that it was time to seriously consider performing a C-section. To her surprise, Edie said no. Edie, it turned out, was terrified of surgery.

Another forty-five minutes of labor had her changing her mind. The woman begged her for either the C-section, or death. Sasha assured her that the C-section was by far the better option.

Just like her labor, Edie's surgery turned out to be not without its tricky moments. The monitor indicated, as they were about to begin, that there was fetal distress. The umbilical cord was wrapped around the baby's neck.

Because of the monitor, Sasha had a neonatal team in place, ready to take the baby the moment he made his entrance into the world. The team did what needed to be done in order to bring him around. There were some very tense moments before the ultimate happy ending.

Sasha found herself on the receiving end of an incredibly fierce hug from Edie's husband once he'd heard his son let out a lusty wail for the first time.

"Thank you. Thank you," Miles had sobbed. "Isn't that the most beautiful sound you've ever heard?" he'd demanded happily.

That would change soon, Sasha thought. She nodded, allowing him to have his revelry without comment. It looked, she thought while pulling off her surgical mask and letting it hang about her neck, as if mother and baby were going to be just fine.

It was a good feeling.

So was finally going home. Sasha made her way to the locker room, her feet shuffling along on the freshly washed floor, too tired to lift them properly.

Stripping off her surgical livery and changing back into her own clothes took more time than she'd anticipated. She hadn't realized just how drained she felt until this very moment. Until the drama was over.

When she was finally in her street clothes, the light green surgical pants and top stuffed into the laundry hamper in the corner, it vaguely occurred to her that she hadn't eaten lunch yet. It was hours past dinnertime, but for some reason, she wasn't hungry.

She supposed that she'd been running on the high she'd sustained in the delivery room. Each and every successful birth left her feeling as if she could walk on clouds for the next hour. The miracle never left her untouched, never grew old.

But its effects were fading now, leaving her craving her bed and sleep. Taking out her purse, she closed the locker with her elbow and began to rummage around, looking for her cell phone. She'd promised Tony to call once baby made three.

Tony had opted to stay late in the squad room, instructing her to give him a call once she was finally finished. For the first time in a week, he hadn't brought her in this morning. She'd gotten the call from Miles Wilson while Tony was in the shower. She'd left him a note and quickly left for the hospital. He hadn't been happy about it when he'd finally connected with her.

She knew that he didn't want her going home alone, but she didn't want to leave her car in the structure for the night. Besides, it had been quiet this last week, with no sign of the killer. She was certain that he had probably been intimidated by the presence of the police and the extra security at the hospital.

Maybe he'd decided it was too dangerous to continue and had aborted any plans to continue his spree, she thought hopefully.

There was no need to bother Tony, she told herself. Closing her cell phone, she dropped it back into her cavernous purse. He'd been looking exhausted himself lately. And that was because he'd been putting in what amounted to double duty. He worked on the case all day and then spent the night with her. Not necessarily sleeping.

She'd woken up several times in the last week to see him sitting in a chair, wide awake. Guarding her. Each time she'd urged him back to bed, and he'd slip in between the sheets. But as soon as she was asleep, she knew he got up again. The man definitely deserved a night off, she decided.

Sasha pulled her coat closer around her as the elevator doors opened on the lower level. Taking a deep breath, she stepped out and then hurried to get to her vehicle. She'd managed to get a parking space near the elevator door this morning. That meant she didn't have to walk too far.

She walked quickly nonetheless, every step she took echoing endlessly through the structure.

The parking facility was far from deserted, even at this time of the evening. But it was filled with vehicles, not people. She would have rather it'd been the other way around.

There it was, she thought, seeing her car in the distance. She already had her keys in her hand and she pointed it toward the vehicle, pressing on the alarm deactivator. She heard a distant "click-click."

"Where's your shadow?"

The voice came from behind her. Sasha swallowed a scream as she swung around. Her heart was pounding in her chest, the sound duplicated and echoing in her ears.

The next moment, she was silently calling herself
an idiot. She found herself looking into the face of
Walter Stevens, the security guard.

She could have hugged him.

Hiking her purse strap up higher on her shoulder,
she slipped her hand over her heart for a second. It
was still pounding hard.

"Oh God, Walter, you really scared me." She took
a deep breath in an attempt to regulate her pulse.
"My shadow?" she asked.

He nodded. "Yeah, that police detective. The one
who's doing the investigation."

She smiled fondly. "You mean Detective Santini."
Funny how her tongue seemed to enjoy wrapping
itself around even his surname. "He's not here
tonight."

Walter looked at her with mild interest. "Off investigating another homicide?"

"Not that I know of. Although I guess he could be,"
she admitted. "I just decided to give him the night off."

The guard nodded, a slight smile forming on his
cherubic face. "Figured you would, eventually. And
that I could wait you out. You're the important one,
you know. The main one."

Sasha was about to ask him what he meant by
that, but the words died in her mouth. She saw him
slip his hand over the hilt of his weapon, his fingers
curling around the handle.

There was a look in his eye that made her blood
suddenly run cold.

Chapter 15

How long did it take for a baby to be born? Tony wondered irritably after checking his watch again. He'd done it so many times in the last couple of hours, he'd lost count. It seemed as if the minute hand had been dipped in molasses. As had this baby who refused to come.

Tony flipped the file closed. Pages slipped out, scattered by the sudden movement.

The last he'd heard from Sasha, or rather, from her nurse who'd said that the doctor had asked her to call, she was going back to the hospital because the woman who'd gone into labor early this morning was *still* in labor.

By now, he knew how Sasha operated. She wasn't

going to leave the hospital until that baby had left the womb. And who knew when that would be?

How long did these things take, anyway? he thought again irritably.

He took a sip of his coffee and frowned. He had this uneasy feeling that refused to recede. It had been riding him all day. The same kind of uneasy feeling he'd had just before he'd learned that Annie had been in a fatal car crash.

He wasn't the kind of man who was superstitious, but something was wrong. Something, but he just couldn't put his finger on it.

Probably being paranoid, he told himself. What was more likely was that Sasha might just get it into her head to go home without him after she was finished, if only to prove that she could. He both loved and hated her independent streak.

One thing he knew for sure, this wasn't the time to prove things. Not with a killer with an agenda loose, he thought darkly.

He heard a chair over to his right squeak. Glancing in that general direction, he saw that Henderson was on his feet.

"Dunno about you, but I'm going to call it a night and go home," Henderson told him. "There's a piece of Boston cream pie in the refrigerator that's been calling to me for the last three hours."

Tony eyed his partner's expanding girth. When they'd first been partnered, Henderson's waist had measured five inches less than it did now. "Tell it that it has the wrong number."

Henderson feigned indignation. "Hey, we all can't be Mr. Universe." He crossed to his desk. "If not for us pudgy, out-of-shape guys, guys like you wouldn't look half as good."

"Whatever."

Sideways logic. It was what Henderson was good at. But right now, he wasn't in the mood to hear it. He was going to call her, Tony decided, taking out his cell phone. And keep calling her until she or someone else around her finally answered.

But before Tony could press the first button to her number, he saw Simon Anderson come barreling into the squad room. The university professor looked as if he was scanning the area. The man stopped just long enough to talk to the first person he encountered. The exchange was too far away to hear, but Tony saw the detective he was talking to point in his direction.

Tony flipped his phone shut, tucked it back into his pocket and braced himself.

"Who the hell do you think you are?" Anderson demanded as he crossed the room, heading straight for him with the rhythm of an oncoming freight train.

"Detective Anthony Santini," Tony replied calmly, then nodded at the battered nameplate sitting on the front of his desk. "It says so right there."

"Don't get smart with me, Santini," Anderson warned. He was as big as Henderson and in far better shape as he eyed the other detective. "I should sue your ass off. Yours and the whole damn police department's."

"The department doesn't have an ass," Tony replied, his tone low. Nothing got his back up more than being threatened. "Want to tell me what the problem is?"

"The 'problem' is that you've been digging into my finances," Anderson shouted. "I just got home and played my messages. There was a call from my bank, saying that the police department requested a statement showing all my transactions for the last year. They're putting a hold on my loan application until this 'matter' is resolved to their satisfaction." By now, he was all but breathing fire. "You have no damn right to be disrupting my life this way."

Tony remained sitting, his face impassive. He was aware that Henderson looked as if he was ready to spring into action at the least sign of trouble.

"It's just routine, Professor Anderson, nothing personal." Each word was slowly measured out. "We wanted to make sure you hadn't made any large withdrawals lately."

"And what business is that of yours if I had?" he wanted to know. "Is this because of my wife, is that it?" He spat out the question contemptuously. "You want to harass someone about knocking off people who were in that operating room, talk to my father-in-law. He's the one who went berserk when Gloria Jean died."

Tony's back straightened. This was the first they'd

heard of the woman having any other family members beyond an apparently not-so-grieving husband. He glanced toward Henderson before looking back at Anderson.

"Her father?"

"Yeah." The strained relationship was evident in the single word. "He's got the brain of a flea, but he took her death hard. Hell, the last I heard, he'd even taken a job at the hospital, saying something about being around the last place where Gloria'd been alive. I figured he went over the deep end."

Tony was on his feet. The uneasy feeling he'd been harboring all day mushroomed into overwhelming proportions. "What's your father-in-law's name?"

"Stevens. Walter Stevens." He looked at them with angry contempt in his eyes. "You going to question him?"

Henderson's mouth dropped open. "Hey, isn't that the—?"

"—security guard who found the first body," Tony ended his partner's thought. Damn, he'd never made the connection. The last names were different and there was no mention made of the relationship.

The back of his neck began to prickle. Tony hurried for the door. He heard Henderson trotting right behind him.

"You go to Stevens' apartment, see if he's there," Tony instructed Henderson.

Henderson stopped and doubled back into the office. The address was noted down in the case file.

"Where are you going to be?" Henderson wanted to know.

Anderson was cursing in the background. Tony ignored him.

"I'm going to the hospital," he told Henderson. "Sasha should have called me by now, or at least answered her cell phone. Something's not right."

Tony called several more times as he sped to the hospital. Frustrated because he kept getting her voice mail, he called the hospital switchboard. They put him through to the maternity ward. The nurse who finally answered informed him that he had "just missed Dr. Pulaski. She just left."

Without calling him, he thought. That meant she was going to take her car back to her apartment.

Why the hell couldn't she listen?

He tried to tell himself that he was allowing his natural pessimism to get the best of him and that everything was all right.

The uneasy feeling was almost unmanageable.

"Walter, why are you doing this?"

Staring down at the small handgun in the security guard's hand, Sasha struggled to sound calm. She had to find a way to stall until someone came. Someone *had* to come. There were so many cars here, waiting for their owners. All she needed was for one of them to arrive. The odds were on her side.

If only luck was.

Walter Stevens tightened his grip on the firearm. "Don't play dumb, Dr. Pulaski. You know why I'm doing this. I'm doing it for Gloria Jean. For my Jeannie." His expression hardened. "Because no one else will. That pompous ass she was married to was glad to be rid of her. All he wanted was to make money off her death." Hatred dripped from every word. It didn't take much of a stretch to envision the last name on Walter Stevens' elimination list. "She was a wonderful, sweet girl. And smart." For a second, he could have been any father, bragging about his daughter. If not for the gun in his hand. "Did you know they made her teacher of the year at her school three years in a row?" And then anger contorted his features. "No, you wouldn't know that. All you saw was someone to practice on."

Was that what he thought? Was that what had festered in his chest, finally prompting the man to go off the deep end? "Walter, it wasn't like that."

Her words seemed to bounce off him. "Sure it was. Otherwise, you would have waited for the specialist to come."

But that was just the point. She had to make him see that. "There wasn't time, Walter. Gloria Jean was going to die if something wasn't done quickly—"

He cut her off, shouting, "She died anyway, didn't she?"

"Yes," she agreed heavily, never taking her eyes off the weapon that was trained on her. "She died anyway." Sasha thought of her parents, of how they would feel if she died here tonight. They'd already been through so much in their lifetime, she wasn't going to let that kind of grief touch them if she could help it. "Walter, we did all we could. You have to believe that. You said that Gloria Jean was a good person—"

"She was," he snapped, fury coming into his eyes.

Sasha kept her voice low, calm. It was the only chance she had. "Then she wouldn't want you to do this. To kill people in her name."

But he shook his head, as if shaking off her words. "I have to. It's all I got left. To make you people pay for killing my little girl." With his left hand, he dug into his pocket. Walter pulled out the carefully folded note he'd printed out on his machine the night after he'd killed Tyler Harris. "Here, take this," he ordered. "Hold it in your hand."

She already knew what it was. "No."

Her refusal incensed him. "I said take it!" he shouted. Taking a step forward, he shoved the paper at her.

Sasha swung her purse at him with all her might. Trying to ward off the block, Walter toppled backwards and fell down. Sasha took off, running as fast as she could back toward where she'd come. If she could just get back to the next level, street level, she'd be all right. There'd be people there. People who would come between her and the deranged security guard.

She just prayed that the man wouldn't have a complete meltdown and start firing at people at random.

Why hadn't she called Tony and waited for him? She made herself a promise to apologize. If she lived long enough.

As she rounded the corner, Sasha heard the squeal of brakes and the sound of a car traveling at a high speed. For a second, she wasn't able to discern if the noise was coming from behind her or in front of her.

Was Walter going to run her down?

And then she saw it, the low-slung sports car coming directly at her. At the last minute, the driver swerved. Tires screeched as the car came to an abrupt, sudden halt.

Tony had always said it could stop on a dime.

Leaning over, he threw open the passenger door. "Sasha, get in!" Tony ordered. The smell of burning rubber permeated the air.

Her heart pounding, she could have cried. Quickly, she did as he instructed, pouring herself into the passenger seat. Idling, the car rumbled, like a bull pawing the ground before charging.

Tony's facade cracked. "Are you all right?" he demanded.

She nodded her head vigorously. She was fine. Now that he was here.

"It's Walter. The guard," she gasped, her lungs aching from the cold air she'd dragged in as she'd run. "He's the hit-and-run victim's father and he's the one who's been killing everyone."

"I know."

He could have kicked himself for not knowing

sooner. For not suspecting. But the man had looked like an overgrown Christmas elf and his suspicions had been lulled. Stupid, Tony reprimanded himself. His oversight had almost gotten Sasha killed.

Tony searched her face, her body, looking for wounds, not bothering to hide his concern. "Did he hurt you?"

Sasha realized that there were tears in the corner of her eyes. Tears of relief, of tension. She blinked them back.

"No, but he was going to. He has a gun, Tony. With a silencer." As she said it, she realized that explained why she hadn't really heard anything that night when Angela had been killed only a few feet away from her. The security guard had used a silencer. "He wanted me to take the note, the same one you found all the other victims holding in their hand." With effort, she forced herself not to think about what had almost happened. And then another thought assailed her. "Tony, he's still out there."

"Yeah, I know." The next moment, Tony got out of the car. He paused only long enough to give her a warning look. "Stay here."

She was about to negate the order. There was no way she was going to let him confront the deranged security guard alone. But before she could get out of the vehicle, Walter suddenly appeared, coming around the corner. His gun was drawn and aimed straight at the windshield.

Sasha cried out a warning. "Tony!"

Tony's weapon was drawn before he ever completed turning away from her. He held it steady in both hands, his eyes trained on the guard. "Drop the gun, Stevens."

Walter stopped walking. "She needs to die, Detective. Just like the others did."

"There'll be no more killing, Stevens." It was an edict, coldly issued. "Now drop the gun," he repeated.

Walter's hands trembled slightly as he continued to hold the weapon. "Don't you see? She killed my daughter."

"She tried to save your daughter," Tony countered. "The hospital records showed that your daughter sustained multiple injuries from the car accident. She was bleeding internally in half a dozen places." He was making it up as he went along, using what he could remember from a Discovery Channel program he'd once seen. "No one could have saved her."

"You're lying!" Walter shouted, growing agitated. The gun shook. "Lying to protect her. She has to die. They all have to die."

Walter let loose with an anguished cry. He raised his gun higher, aiming it straight at Sasha's head. Uttering a curse, Tony fired. The bullet struck Walter dead center in the forehead. Just the way the guard had executed all the other victims.

A second shot rang out, this one coming from Walter's gun. The security guard fired the weapon as he went down, a stunned expression frozen into his features.

Sasha bolted from the shelter of the vehicle, rounding the engine until she was next to Tony's side. Frantically, she scanned him for any signs of a wound.

"Are you all right?"

Tony nodded. "Yeah."

She closed her eyes, uttering a silent prayer of thanks. When she opened them again, Sasha crossed to the body lying on the ground a few feet away from them.

"He's dead, Sasha," Tony called after her. He holstered his weapon, knowing he was going to have to turn it into Internal Affairs until all the facts about the shooting were duly taken into account.

Sasha felt the man's neck for a pulse anyway. There was none. Steeling herself, she passed a hand over Walter's lifeless eyes, closing them. "I had to be sure."

Tony joined her and slipped an arm around her shoulders. She was trembling, he realized, even though she was struggling not to show any emotion. "To stop the nightmares?" he guessed.

"Because I'm a doctor," she corrected. "And if he was alive, I took an oath to keep him that way."

Tony thought that was rather ironic, seeing as how the man had been trying to kill her. In her position, he didn't know if he would have been able to think that way. Not about someone who had gone to such lengths to try to eliminate him.

A sigh shuddered its way out of his throat as he placed a call in to dispatch to apprise them of the situation.

He was vaguely aware that the uneasy feeling haunting him all day was gone.

"I can't believe it's really over."

Sasha sank down on a stool beside Tony, a mug of hot tea in her hand. It was more than three hours later and they were finally in her apartment. She'd gone to the police station with him, insisting on giving her statement now instead of in the morning the way he'd suggested. There was no way she was going to allow this to linger. She'd wanted to purge as much of the incident as she could before going home.

The moment she and Tony had walked into the apartment, her sisters had surrounded her. They'd fussed over her as much as she would allow them to. She'd answered their questions and assured them more than once that she was all right. Tony was about to take his leave when she'd stopped him, asking him to remain a few more minutes.

That had been Natalya and Kady's cue. To their credit, they'd taken it quickly and retreated back into the bedrooms from which they'd emerged.

Natalya had paused to give her an extra hard hug. "We'll figure out how to sugarcoat this for Mama and Daddy in the morning," she whispered. All three of them knew that their parents would be after them to move back home.

Sasha had smiled and nodded. "I'd appreciate the help." Natalya had always been the more creative one of the three.

Tony had sat quietly, studying his coffee mug until her sisters finally left them alone. And then he looked at her, trying not to think of the way things could have gone tonight. Focusing only on the fact that she was alive and out of danger.

"It'll take some time for you to get it out of your system," he warned. "Sometimes our emotions won't accept what our minds tell us is really true."

She raised her eyes to his. Her intuition told her that he wasn't referring to the fact that there was no more need to be afraid. "You're talking about your wife, aren't you?"

He began to deny it, then shrugged. Wasn't much point in doing that. She seemed to be able to see right through him. The next moment, he realized that that didn't scare him any more. "Among other things."

She smiled, affection in her eyes. "I had no idea you could wax so poetic."

He laughed shortly. That wasn't what some people called it. "I have my moments."

"Yes," she said softly, running the back of her hand across his cheek, creating all sorts of tidal waves inside his stomach, "I know."

Tony knew he should be leaving. Closing this chapter of his life and going back to the routine that he knew best. Being a cop. He didn't belong in her life. She was too good and he was too jaded.

And yet, he found himself reaching for her. With his arm hooked around her waist, he drew her onto his lap. She nestled in, adding more friction to the already existing tidal waves.

"I guess you'll be relieved not to be needing a bodyguard anymore."

He couldn't quite read the expression on her face. It was a cross between whimsical and thoughtful.

"Oh, I don't know about that. New York City is a pretty dangerous place at times. A woman can't be too careful these days." And then she smiled into his eyes. "A little extra protection would be very welcome."

He shouldn't be thinking what he was thinking. Shouldn't allow himself to grow optimistic. But he did. "It would?"

"Uh-huh." She only half succeeded in looking serious. "Any idea where I might be able to find that kind of protection?" She laced her fingers around his neck. "The kind that would be available at odd hours of the day or night?"

Tony nodded, never taking his eyes off her face. "I think I know just the guy."

Sasha's smile widened. "I was hoping you'd say that."

He never missed a beat. "Henderson's been looking to pick up a little extra cash."

About to kiss him, Sasha pulled her head back. "Henderson?"

"Yeah." And then, unable to help himself, Tony grinned. "I'm just going to have to tell him to find someone else to guard. That this body," he tucked his hands around her, "is spoken for."

He'd had her going for a second. Paying him back, Sasha whacked his shoulder with the flat of her hand. He looked at her in surprise. "That's for Henderson."

He laughed, pulling her even closer. "I'll deliver it when I get a chance."

He didn't make it sound as if he was going anywhere anytime soon. "Planning to be busy for a while?"

"For a very long while," he told her, as he began to lower his mouth to hers. "Say like the next ten or twenty years."

Sasha looked at him pointedly. "Ten or twenty years? That's all?"

"We'll negotiate."

Tony tasted her laugh against his lips and felt rays of hope and sunshine spread out all through him as he deepened the kiss.

In his mind, he amended the length of time to forever.

*Silhouette® Romantic Suspense
keeps getting hotter!*

Turn the page for a sneak preview of
New York Times *bestselling author
Beverly Barton's latest title from*
THE PROTECTORS *miniseries.*

*HIS ONLY OBSESSION
by Beverly Barton*

*On sale March 2007
wherever books are sold.*

Gwen took a taxi to the Yellow Parrot, and with each passing block she grew more tense. It didn't take a rocket scientist to figure out that this dive was in the worst part of town. Gwen had learned to take care of herself, but the minute she entered the bar, she realized that a smart woman would have brought a gun with her. The interior was hot, smelly and dirty, and the air was so smoky that it looked as if a pea soup fog had settled inside the building. Before she had gone three feet, an old drunk came up to her and asked for money. Sidestepping him, she searched for someone who looked as if he or she might actually work here, someone other than the prostitutes who were trolling for customers.

After fending off a couple of grasping young men and ignoring several vulgar propositions in an odd mixture of Spanish and English, Gwen found the bar. She ordered a beer from the burly, bearded bartender. When he set the beer in front of her, she took the opportunity to speak to him.

"I'm looking for a man. An older American man, in his seventies. He was probably with a younger woman. This man is my father and—"

"*No hablo inglés.*"

"Oh." He didn't speak English and she didn't speak Spanish. Now what?

While she was considering her options, Gwen noticed a young man in skintight black pants and an open black shirt, easing closer and closer to her as he made his way past the other men at the bar.

Great. That was all she needed—some horny young guy mistaking her for a prostitute.

"*Señorita.*" His voice was softly accented and slightly slurred. His breath smelled of liquor. "You are all alone, *sí?*"

"Please, go away," Gwen said. "I'm not interested."

He laughed, as if he found her attitude amusing. "Then it is for me to make you interested. I am Marco. And you are…?"

"Leaving," Gwen said.

She realized it had been a mistake to come here alone tonight. Any effort to unearth information about her father in a place like this was probably pointless. She would do better to come back tomorrow and try to speak to the owner. But when she tried to move past her ardent young suitor, he reached out and grabbed her arm. She tensed.

Looking him right in the eyes, she told him, "Let go of me. Right now."

"But you cannot leave. The night is young."

Gwen tugged on her arm, trying to break free. He tightened his hold, his fingers biting into her flesh. With her heart beating rapidly as her basic fight-or-flight instinct kicked in, she glared at the man.

"I'm going to ask you one more time to let me go."

Grinning smugly, he grabbed her other arm, holding her in place.

Suddenly, seemingly from out of nowhere, a big hand clamped down on Marco's shoulder, jerked him back and spun him around. Suddenly free, Gwen swayed slightly but managed to retain her balance as she watched in amazement as a tall, lanky man in jeans and cowboy boots shoved her would-be suitor up against the bar.

"I believe the lady asked you real nice to let her go," the man said, in a deep Texas drawl. "Where I come from, a gentleman respects a lady's wishes."

Marco grumbled something unintelligible in Spanish. Probably cursing, Gwen thought. Or maybe praying. If she were Marco, she would be praying that the big, rugged American wouldn't beat her to a pulp.

Apparently Marco was not as smart as she was. When the Texan released him, he came at her rescuer, obviously intending to fight him. The Texan took Marco out with two swift punches, sending the younger man to the floor. Gwen glanced down at where Marco lay sprawled flat on his back, unconscious.

Her hero turned to her. "Ma'am, are you all right?"

She nodded. The man was about six-two, with a sunburned tan, sun-streaked brown hair and azure-blue eyes.

"What's a lady like you doing in a place like this?" he asked.

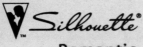
Romantic
SUSPENSE

Excitement, danger and passion guaranteed!

Same great authors and riveting editorial
you've come to know and love
from Silhouette Intimate Moments.

> *New York Times*
> bestselling author
> Beverly Barton
> is back with the
> latest installment
> in her popular
> miniseries,
> The Protectors.
> HIS ONLY
> OBSESSION
> is available
> next month from
> Silhouette®
> Romantic Suspense

Look for it wherever you buy books!

Visit Silhouette Books at www.eHarlequin.com   SRSBB27525

This February…

Catch NASCAR Superstar **Carl Edwards** *in*
SPEED DATING!

Kendall assesses risk for a living—
so she's the last person you'd
expect to see on the arm of a
race-car driver who thrives on the
unpredictable. But when a bizarre
turn of events—and NASCAR
hotshot Dylan Hargreave—inspire
her to trade in her ever-so-structured
existence for "life in the fast lane"
she starts to feel she might be
on to something!

Collect all 4 debut novels in the Harlequin NASCAR series.

SPEED DATING
by *USA TODAY* bestselling author
Nancy Warren

THUNDERSTRUCK
by Roxanne St. Claire

HEARTS UNDER CAUTION
by Gina Wilkins

DANGER ZONE
by Debra Webb

On sale February 2007

www.eHarlequin.com

NASCARFEB

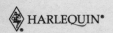

EVERLASTING LOVE™

Every great love has a story to tell™

Save $1.⁰⁰ off

the purchase of
any Harlequin
Everlasting Love novel

Coupon valid from January 1, 2007
until April 30, 2007.

Valid at retail outlets in the U.S. only.
Limit one coupon per customer.

RETAILER: Harlequin Enterprises Limited will pay the face value of this coupon plus
8¢ if submitted by the customer for this product only. Any other use constitutes fraud.
Coupon is nonassignable. Void if taxed, prohibited or restricted by law. Consumer
must pay any government taxes. Void if copied. For reimbursement submit coupons
and proof of sales directly to: Harlequin Enterprises Ltd., P.O. Box 880478, El Paso,
TX 88588-0478, U.S.A. Cash value 1/100¢. Valid in the U.S. only. ® is a trademark of
Harlequin Enterprises Ltd. Trademarks marked with ® are registered in the United
States and/or other countries.

5 65373 00076 2   (8100) 0 11302

HEUSCPN0407

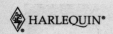

HARLEQUIN®

EVERLASTING LOVE™

Every great love has a story to tell™

Save $1.⁰⁰ off

the purchase of
any Harlequin
Everlasting Love novel

Coupon valid from January 1, 2007
until April 30, 2007.

Valid at retail outlets in Canada only.
Limit one coupon per customer.

RETAILER: Harlequin Enterprises Limited will pay the face value of this coupon plus 10.25¢ if submitted by the customer for this product only. Any other use constitutes fraud. Coupon is nonassignable. Void if taxed, prohibited or restricted by law. Consumer must pay any government taxes. Void if copied. Nielsen Clearing House customers submit coupons and proof of sales to: Harlequin Enterprises Ltd. P.O. Box 3000, Saint John, N.B. E2L 4L3. Non–NCH retailer—for reimbursement submit coupons and proof of sales directly to: Harlequin Enterprises Ltd., Retail Marketing Department, 225 Duncan Mill Rd., Don Mills, Ontario M3B 3K9, Canada. Valid in Canada only. ® is a trademark of Harlequin Enterprises Ltd. Trademarks marked with ® are registered in the United States and/or other countries.

52607370

HECDNCPN0407

Hearts racing
Blood pumping
Pulses accelerating

**Falling in love can be
a blur...especially at**
180 mph!

**So if you crave the thrill
of the chase—on and off
the track—you'll love**

SPEED DATING
by **Nancy Warren!**

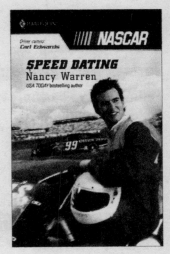

Receive $1.⁰⁰ off
SPEED DATING
or any other Harlequin NASCAR book.

Coupon expires December 31, 2007. Redeemable at participating retail
outlets in the U.S. only. Limit one coupon per customer.

RETAILER: Harlequin Enterprises Ltd. will pay the face value of this coupon plus
8 cents if submitted by the customer for this specified product only. Any other use
constitutes fraud. Coupon is nonassignable. Void if taxed, prohibited or restricted by
law. Void if copied. Consumer must pay for any government taxes. Mail to Harlequin
Enterprises Ltd., P.O. Box 880478, El Paso, TX 88588-0478, U.S.A. Cash value 1/100
cents. Limit one coupon per customer. Valid in the U.S. only.

113854

5 65373 00076 2   (8100) 0 11385

NASCPNUS

Hearts racing
Blood pumping
Pulses accelerating

Falling in love can be a blur...especially at **180 mph!**

So if you crave the thrill of the chase—on and off the track—you'll love

SPEED DATING by Nancy Warren!

Receive $1.⁰⁰ off

SPEED DATING
or any other Harlequin NASCAR book.

Coupon expires December 31, 2007. Redeemable at participating retail outlets in Canada only. Limit one coupon per customer.

RETAILER: Harlequin Enterprises Ltd. will pay the face value of this coupon plus 10.25¢ if submitted by the customer for this product only. Any other use constitutes fraud. Coupon is nonassignable. Void if taxed, prohibited or restricted by law. Consumer must pay any government taxes. Void if copied. Nielson Clearing House customers submit coupons and proof of sales to: Harlequin Enterprises Ltd., P.O. Box 3000, Saint John, NB E2L 4L3. Non-NCH retailer—for reimbursement submit coupons and proof of sales directly to: Harlequin Enterprises Ltd., Retail Marketing Department, 225 Duncan Mill Rd., Don Mills, Ontario M3B 3K9, Canada. Valid in Canada only. ® is a trademark of Harlequin Enterprises Ltd. Trademarks marked with ® are registered in the United States and/or other countries.

52607628

NASCPNCDN

REQUEST YOUR FREE BOOKS!

2 FREE NOVELS PLUS 2 FREE GIFTS!

Silhouette® Romantic

SUSPENSE

Sparked by Danger, Fueled by Passion!

YES! Please send me 2 FREE Silhouette® Romantic Suspense novels and my 2 FREE gifts. After receiving them, if I don't wish to receive any more books, I can return the shipping statement marked "cancel." If I don't cancel, I will receive 4 brand-new novels every month and be billed just $4.24 per book in the U.S., or $4.99 per book in Canada, plus 25¢ shipping and handling per book plus applicable taxes, if any*. That's a savings of at least 15% off the cover price! I understand that accepting the 2 free books and gifts places me under no obligation to buy anything. I can always return a shipment and cancel at any time. Even if I never buy another book from Silhouette, the two free books and gifts are mine to keep forever.

240 SDN EEX6 340 SDN EEYJ

Name	(PLEASE PRINT)

Address	Apt. #

City	State/Prov.	Zip/Postal Code

Signature (if under 18, a parent or guardian must sign)

Mail to the **Silhouette Reader Service™**:
IN U.S.A.: P.O. Box 1867, Buffalo, NY 14240-1867
IN CANADA: P.O. Box 609, Fort Erie, Ontario L2A 5X3

Not valid to current Silhouette Intimate Moments subscribers.

Want to try two free books from another line?
Call 1-800-873-8635 or visit www.morefreebooks.com.

* Terms and prices subject to change without notice. NY residents add applicable sales tax. Canadian residents will be charged applicable provincial taxes and GST. This offer is limited to one order per household. All orders subject to approval. Credit or debit balances in a customer's account(s) may be offset by any other outstanding balance owed by or to the customer. Please allow 4 to 6 weeks for delivery.

Your Privacy: Silhouette is committed to protecting your privacy. Our Privacy Policy is available online at www.eHarlequin.com or upon request from the Reader Service. From time to time we make our lists of customers available to reputable firms who may have a product or service of interest to you. If you would prefer we not share your name and address, please check here. ☐

SRS07

Silhouette®

Romantic

SUSPENSE

COMING NEXT MONTH

#1455 HIS ONLY OBSESSION—Beverly Barton
The Protectors
After rescuing the alluring Dr. Gwen Arnell, Dundee agent Will Pierce
realizes that they are both searching for the same man. Together
they set sail, island-hopping in their quest to find their target and a
mysterious youth serum…while battling an attraction neither can deny.

#1456 MISSION: M.D.—Linda Turner
Turning Points
Rachel Martin is dying to seduce the gorgeous doctor who lives next
door, but a stalker wants to stop her. Will Rachel be able to keep her
distance despite the growing desire she feels for her neighbor?

#1457 SHADOW SURRENDER—Linda Conrad
Night Guardians
Special Agent Teal Benaly finds dangers hidden at every turn as she
sets out to investigate a strange murder on the Navajo reservation. But
nothing holds the potential danger she finds in the arms of the dark
stranger sent to protect her.

#1458 ONE HOT TARGET—Diane Pershing
When an innocent woman dies, police believe that Carmen Coyle
might have been the potential target. With the help of her lawyer-
friend JR Ellis, Carmen tries to track down possible leads—and resist
the temptation to explore a more personal relationship with JR.

SRSCNM0207